OLD IRON GLOVE

By the Author of

OLD IRON GLOVE

by JOE ARCHIBALD

MACRAE SMITH COMPANY • Philadelphia

OLD IRON GLOVE

1 ☻

AT BRIGGS STADIUM IN DETROIT THE PITCHERS WERE IN control and were working as hot as the sun. They were nipping the corners of the plate with their curves, and their fast balls were alive as they steamed by the hitters. It was the last half of the sixth inning between the Detroit Cougars and the New York Titans, and the big crowd, bored by the tight mound duel, clamored for some stickwork. As each Cougar hitter stepped up to the plate he was stung by the harsh, relentless abuse from the grandstand hecklers.

Jim Bruckner sat in a corner of the Detroit dugout near the bat rack, arms folded, knees crossed, his angular bronzed face pulled out of shape by a quid of tobacco. He was glad Mike Strager was not using him today, as he watched the young fifteen-thousand-dollar bonus beauty, Ron Kershaw, step up to face New York's lefty, Ed Ridel. One Cougar was out and the base paths were clear.

"Get us going, kid!" the Cougar manager yelled through cupped hands, and Jim's wide mouth curled up at one corner. Kershaw was a tall, broad-shouldered kid as green as the grass on a putting green, and the Cougars had signed him off a college campus. The new breed, Jim Bruckner growled to himself —one of the darlings of the accursed first year rule that meant the skids for many a veteran—the overpolite, polished, All-

American boy, who thought spikes were used only to dig a firmer foothold in the batter's box.

Jim watched Ridel closely, certain the Titan had been throwing a spitter along with his assortment of curves, sliders, and change-ups. Sure, most pitchers went to their mouths and wet their fingers and then wiped the fingers off on their uniforms, but who could prove they dried clean the fingers that were wet? No curve or sinker can possibly break as sharply as a spitter. It comes in as if it is rolling off a table.

Ridel got his first pitch below Kershaw's knees, and then threw his fast ball right past the rookie. His curve hung, and the kid fouled it off into the crowd back of third. Kershaw stepped out and looked up the third base line toward the Cougar coach, Josh Dillon, and a fan roared, "That's it, rookie; give him the bat and let him hit!"

Jim could see the batter's ears redden as the youngster dug in once more. A pitch came in tight and he staggered backward, nearly losing his footing. When Kershaw stepped out and picked up some dirt to grind the scare-sweat out of the palms of his hands, the Titan bench poured it on him. With the count even, Ridel reared back and fired the hard one, too high, and the string had run out. The Titan pitcher rubbed up the ball and eyed the Cougar in the on-deck circle. Hank Bruda had eleven homers during the young season. Ridel wanted first base unoccupied when the slugger came up.

Ridel's fingers brushed across his mouth and across the front of his sweat-soaked uniform. He looked in, nodded, wound up and threw. Kershaw took a full cut and missed the sharp, breaking curve by at least a foot. The wolves in the stands chewed the rookie out all the way to the dugout. Jim shouted above the partisan crowd's roar of welcome to Bruda, "If that wasn't a spitter, my aunt Hattie is an astronaut! Have they made that pitch legal since yesterday?"

Mike Strager turned away from the dugout steps and threw

the veteran first baseman-outfielder a look of disapproval from under his bushy eyebrows.

Too bad, Mr. Strager, you just haven't got the guts to question anything the pin-stripers do. They're the proud Titans, the perennial flag-winners. As he watched Ridel work on Hank Bruda he thought of the cockeyed legend that told of the magic in the New York uniforms. Just put a Titan pair of pants and a baseball shirt on a mediocre outcast from any other ball club and he would turn into a shining star overnight. In Jim's book it was plain hogwash, and he fondly recollected, as he followed the flight of a foul hit by Bruda out of the park, that a certain St. Louis National ball club had once run the Titans ragged in a certain World Series.

"Get a good one, Hank," Stan Jaciuk, the Cougar left fielder, yelled in Jim's ear. Bruda got it, and rammed a double off the fence in right, the crowd coming up and roaring for the Cougars to break the deadlock. Bert Alschul, another power hitter, dug in, and Ridel looked out at the stirring Titan bullpen as he rubbed up a new ball.

"Send him to the showers, Bert!" Jim yelled. "Drive it down his throat." An old hate for the New Yorkers built up inside him. He turned his saltiest vocabulary loose on Ridel until even some of the Cougars winced. Strager leveled his eyes at him. "Hold it down, Bruckner! There's a limit."

Nuts, Strager. Why don't you go out there and pat Ridel on the back? There's only one way to beat the pin-stripers, and it's in a book, Mike. I'll show it to you sometime.

Alschul, with the count three balls and one strike, slammed a grounder to deep short that the Titan fielder bobbled long enough to allow Bruda to go to third and Alschul to first; and Briggs Stadium began to rock. Ridel kicked dirt from the mound and pounded the ball in the pocket of his glove. The dusky Jeremiah Jones stepped in and drove a long fly ball to center, Hank Bruda strolling in from third after the catch.

Jeremiah's brother, Zach, the Cougar second baseman, ended the inning by fouling out to the Titan backstop.

Jim sat back and watched Strager's right-hander, Ed Stangaard, labor against the top third of the Titan batting order in the first half of the seventh. It was time, he mused, for the New Yorkers' "five o'clock lightning." Stangaard, wilting under the pressure of the tight game and the heat, lost the Titan leadoff man, Riseman, after running the count full. Lubec, the Titan right fielder, took a pitch into the dirt, fouled one off, then belted Stangaard's change-up into right field, sending Riseman to third. Strager left the dugout when Stangaard threw two bad pitches in at the Titan slugger, Nick Parisi. At the mound he took the ball from the right hander and signaled for a southpaw to come out of the bullpen.

The same old script, Jim Bruckner told himself, and shook his head in disgust. You held the star-studded Titans for a few innings, then boom! They wore other teams down with their psychological hooey and the power they never seemed to lack, decade after decade. That's what the writers said. Jim chose to believe that most teams "choked up" in the presence of the American League monopoly, that they were inclined to pull their punches against the highly paid New York pennant-winning machine. Oh, for another Alley Gang out of St. Louis or anywhere else. While the new Cougar pitcher, Lenny Dee, took the long walk in, Jim's mind sped quickly back over the past. More than eleven years in baseball were behind him, seven of them, for the most part, having been spent in the minors from Class B to Class AAA. His two best years had been with the Cleveland Chiefs, and it had seemed that he would enjoy a long career in the lake city until he'd hurt his knee banging against the right field wall in Baltimore.

Before the knee had mended sufficiently to allow him to play every day, he had been turned loose to make way for a younger and sounder body. After hitting close to .300 with

10

Dallas he had been brought back to the big time by the Boston Pilgrims; and just as it seemed he would stay on in the Hub, the haunting youth movement followed him there and sent him packing once more. He hit .296 with Salt Lake, and a Titan scout, seeking outfield insurance for the New Yorkers, had come to the park the day he'd hit a double and two singles. The report the scout had turned in came back to him by a devious route. "Bruckner's a fair enough hitter, but he'll give the other side as many runs with his 'iron' glove as he drives in with his bat. He hasn't the temperament of a New York Titan."

Watching Dee finish his warm-up, Jim admitted he was no scintillating fielder. He could not discount his thirty years, for at that age a man is really pushing sixty, in the world of baseball. There were traces of crows' feet at the corners of his dark eyes, and a parenthesis was forming at each side of his mouth. He could count one blessing: there was no gray in his close-cropped dark hair.

He watched Parisi dig in against Strager's relief hurler, still remembering and inwardly writhing over that tag line in the Titan scout's report. He knew what the man really meant. *Bruckner is a roughneck. We don't want his type on the Titans.*

Before the start of the game, with the Cougars taking batting practice, the pin-stripers from New York had worked him over from their bench, and he had given it back to them in spades, and once it seemed the Titan manager, George Phipps, was on the verge of coming out to use weapons heavier than words. "Come on, Phippsy!" Jim had shouted for many in the front seats to hear, "I'll knock you loose from your pin-stripes!"

He turned his attention to the action once more. Dee was behind on Parisi three and nothing, and the fans were squirming in their seats. Parisi watched a strike go by, then checked with the Titan coach off third. He had the green light. He swung on the next pitch and drove it to deep left, where Jeremiah Jones finally caught up with the ball close to the barrier. Riseman scored for New York, and Lubec tagged up and then raced to second. The noise in the stadium swelled as the Titan cleanup hitter, who hit from both sides, stepped in to face Dee.

Jim watched Ernie Brossett get a foothold, denying the slightest feeling of envy as the hundred-thousand-dollar slugger cocked his bat. Fifty-three home runs last year, a .351 batting average.

Lenny Dee kept his pitches in tight on Brossett's fists, the second pitch too tight. The count even, he gave the hitter a big motion and then pulled the string. Brossett uncoiled and slammed the half speed pitch down the alley between right and center for a triple and the Titans went out in front, 2-1. With the New York catcher, Sam Ricci, moving in, Strager went out and yanked his left-hander, and called for his ace fireman, Pedro Camacho.

Al Udane, a reserve outfielder, came away from the water cooler. He had been around for a long time. He took off his cap, mopped a bald spot with a towel and threw the towel away. He grinned down at Jim. "What did you come back for, Bruckner?"

"Why do you hang on, Al?"

"Well, I figure the pitchers get no smarter and I get no dumber," Udane said, and grinned wide. "What other work could I get? The only sheepskin I ever saw was still on the animal."

Jim nodded, his face sober. The educational kick had permeated the business of baseball. A lot of college boys were working on theses during the plane trips and between doubleheaders. Why, they had a league in operation in the midwest composed of college stars, and in lieu of salaries they were given jobs in the towns involved at prevailing rates of pay. The sandlot teen-ager, he figured—the kid who had little or no chance to go to college—had been sandbagged.

12

His eyes were a little bleak and the hands on his knees balled into fists as he watched Camacho try to get the side out. Pedro fired a pitch into the dirt that Bert Alschul could not come up with, and Brossett raced in with the Titans' third run.

"Half the time," Jim ground out, "those guys don't beat anybody. They let you beat yourselves!"

Strager walked up and down, hands shoved into the back pockets of his baggy pants, muttering under his breath. A few agonizing minutes later, Pedro, after loading the bases, got the Titan pitcher to bang into a double play.

The dyed-in-the-wool bleacher fans gave Brossett some applause when he took his place in center field, and Jim ground his teeth. Detroit fans were giving their sixth place team a real barbering as it spilled into the dugout. In the old days, he knew, home fans would have been tempted to shoot Brossett. One of the old Alley Gang would have tried to spike him while he rounded the bases. The world had gone soft and baseball along with it. No wonder Krushy dared to shout his mouth off and threaten to bury the Western world. Jim spat to the concrete.

Jim got up from the bench as a pinch hitter left the dugout to hit for Camacho. He read little sympathy in the row of sunburned, sweaty Cougar faces, and expected none. If he fired them up at times, it was not with his winning personality but with his double-edged taunts. From the time he had thrown away his comic books he had been something of a lone wolf, in and out of baseball. The struggle to survive strictly on his own had given him little opportunity to embrace the social graces, and he stubbornly refused to accept the new image of the professional baseball player.

Duke McIver, a rookie infielder, tried to bunt himself on but was thrown out on a great play by the New York third baseman. Tex Loun and Jaciuk struck out, and the fans booed

13

the Cougars as they took the field again. Strager had his "junk man," Wes Ardwell, on the mound; and the tail end of the Titan batting order, having seen fast stuff for most of the afternoon, were off on their timing, swinging helplessly at Ardwell's tantalizing delivery. They went down in order, and the home crowd yelled for the Cougars to come alive as they came in to hit.

Kershaw, first up, hung in against Ridel, spraying foul balls everywhere after the count had run to three and two. He walked, and the crowd buzzed. Jim yelled for Bruda to lose one as the heavy hitter took his stance at the plate. Hank swung hard at Ridel's first pitch and sent it sky-high over the infield, throwing his bat away in disgust as he ran toward first. The Titan shortstop camped under the pop-up and let it settle in his glove. With Alschul up and Jeremiah Jones on deck, Ridel wild-pitched, Kershaw legging it for the pick-up spot.

The fans set up a rhythmic clapping of hands and stamping of feet, and a contingent of cub scouts up in the stands droned out the familiar chant, "We wa-a-ant a hit! We wa-a-a-ant a hit!" Jim Bruckner came up yelling with the rest of the Cougars when Alschul lined a hit betwen first and second, Kershaw scoring the second run for Detroit. Activity began in the visitors' bullpen, and Jim led the jockeying of the ruffled Titan mound ace.

"You smell from here, Ridel! You need a shower! You run out of spit, Buster?"

Even the most retiring of the Cougars added their verbal darts to the barrage showering the Titan lefty. The crowd's racket drowned out what Strager was saying to Zach Jones, who was headed for the hitter's circle. The colored player kept on walking, knelt down in the on-deck station and yelled for his brother Jeremiah to cream one into orbit. Big Jerry worked a tiring Ridel to a three balls and one strike count, then shifted his feet and drilled a fast ball into right for a clean single, sending Alschul around to third.

14

Strager's voice sounded close to Jim Bruckner's ear. "Get yourself a bat. Let's see how much you hate the Titans."

Zach Jones came back into the dugout, threw Strager a resentful glance, and shoved his bat into the rack.

The crowd gave Jim an ovation when he left the dugout and a small smile curled his lips. Writers had often impressed upon the minds of the cash customers that his appearance alone suggested and promised excitement whether he delivered or not. Bruckner, they wrote, made things happen. He was a time bomb always expected to explode, a throwback from the days of the trolley cars and the five-cent hot dog. He reveled in the big hand the fans gave him, one that almost drowned out the public address system.

On his way to the plate he glanced toward the visitors' dugout and spat into the dirt, letting their verbal strafing wash in and over him. Digging in, he glanced at the faces of the New York infield, and immediately caught the ragged edge of their mood. The Titans had reason to remember Jim Bruckner. In the Yankee Stadium, while with the Pilgrims, he had come into the plate, spikes high, and had hit the Titan catcher like a bulldozer, knocked the man ten feet back of the plate and broken his leg.

Ricci, the Titan receiver, was not forgetting. He had been out of action for most of that year. "We hoped you'd be back, Bruckner," he said coldly. "What are they payin' for retreads in Detroit?"

"You came F.O.B., I know," Jim parried, and picked up some dirt. "Full of bull."

Ridel checked Alschul edging off third, then tried to pick Jones off first with the quick motion that had made him famous. He fired the ball to the initial sack again, and the fans began to ride him, screaming their impatience. The tension built up. The Titan bench became more abusive, and even the hot dog, beverage and peanut butchers in the stands closed up shop for the moment.

Jim clamped his teeth down hard on his chew of tobacco, dead certain he was to get the full treatment.

Ridel fired a fast ball below Jim's knees, and Ricci walked halfway to the mound to fire the ball back. The Titan pitcher let the hitter wait. He went to the rosin bag, straightened out his pant legs, took off his cap and sleeved the sweat off his brow. A stout-lunged fan shouted, "Okay, they've taken your picture. Throw it, you bum!"

Ridel got set, then turned a fireball loose that came straight at Jim's head. He hit the dirt with only a split second to spare, and an angry roar filled the stadium. A small grin on his face, Jim picked himself up, banged dirt from his uniform and stared out at Ridel. His anger deepened as the Titan pitcher turned his back on him and looked out at his defense. He looked at Ricci's face behind the steel mask and saw the cold smile on the catcher's face. The umpire seemed unconcerned.

All right, let's play it your way, Jim growled to himself, and got a firm foothold again. Ridel's pitch came in wide of the plate, but Jim took a full cut, letting the bat slip out of his hands. It sailed straight at the Titan pitcher, who had to dive off the mound to save himself from getting skulled, and the fans came off their seats screaming.

"Sorry, it slipped," Jim called out, his eyes daring the umpire to disagree. "Like Ridel's pitch."

The Titan shortstop retrieved the bat near the keystone sack and walked toward the mound where Ridel rested on one knee, his face the color of wood ash. The New York first and third basemen joined Ricci in the center of the diamond, and suddenly tempers flared when the Titan shortstop hurled the bat toward the mocking Detroit dugout. The Cougars came out onto the field, snarling, just as Jim ducked a punch thrown at him by Ricci. He dove in at the big backstop, wrapped his arms around him and wrestled him to the ground. He was banging Ricci's face against the turf when half a dozen pairs of

16

hands tore him loose. The umpires and the Briggs Stadium police forced finally restored order, the crowd soundly booing their efforts. An argument between Strager, Phipps and the men in blue as to who would be thrown out of the game immediately followed, and the Cougar manager came out ahead. Ricci, along with the New York shortstop, was ordered to the showers, and then Phipps kicked dirt against the plate ump's trousers and was also given the heave. Jim's plea had been self-defense.

Comparative quiet restored, Ridel began to work again. Shaken up, he got himself into the three and two situation and fired his fast ball. It was only half alive and Jim nailed it just inside the third-base sack, the Titan hot corner man making a futile stab at it. The ball rolled all the way to the left field corner, and Alschul and Jones wheeled around to score on the two-base knock. Detroit, 4; Titans, 3. New York's acting manager lost no time getting to the mound. He signaled the bullpen for a right-hander.

The Titan infielders let Jim Bruckner know what he could expect the rest of the summer as he stood on second and watched the New York fireman stroll in. He gave the particularly offensive reserve Titan shortstop an icy grin. "Why, I thought you pin-stripers were model gentlemen," he threw at the man, "the elite of baseball. Yeah, like beauty, your manners are only skin deep." He laughed. "You, Kaula, have a B.A. degree from some place like Yoohoo U. It sure can't mean a batting average. Guess you know where the bodies are buried, huh?"

Kaula moved toward him, shoving his glove into his back pocket. "You big crud, Bruckner. I'll take these glasses off and——"

The third base umpire, who had been talking to the Cougar coach, came running. "All right, break it up!" he ordered. "Bruckner, you hold it down!"

"Sure, Bill. I didn't know these boys were so sensitive."

The veteran Titan relief pitcher, Howitt, retired the next two Cougars and left Jim stranded at second. When he reached the dugout, Strager said, "You can call it a day, Bruckner. Nice work."

Jim nodded. He was on his way out of the steamy dugout when Strager called after him. "But one thing I know. You won't ever qualify for the Peace Corps."

The laughter from the other benchwarmers did not come from down deep, for Jim Bruckner had never come within a country mile of winning a popularity contest. They resented his oft-repeated contention that the business side of baseball had taken a great chunk of glamour out of the sport, that the old hustle, the all-consuming will to win despite the size of a player's salary check, was gone. He had given his unvarnished opinion to the writers back in the spring training camp. "Sure, I'm grateful to the Detroit club for bringing me back from Omaha," he'd said. "They came after me—I didn't go to them —and maybe they figured to draw fans from the crumby sections of the city to root for one of their kind."

In the clubhouse he stripped off his uniform, had a shower, wrapped a towel around himself and waited for the other players to come in. The TV showed that the game was over and the crowd was swarming over the infield, and it was a safe bet the Cougars had made the one-run lead stand up. He was kidding with Barney Cott, the equipment man, when the soggy Detroit club poured into the dressing room, still loud in their praise of Old Wes Ardwell's relief pitching. Charlie Overman, utility outfielder, the oldest player on the club, eyed his roommate with a dry grin. "Strager's getting a cordon of cops to get you back to the hotel in one piece, Jim."

"Are you kidding? Strager would furnish the Titans the brass knuckles." He got up, wrapped a towel more securely around his middle, and sought out the trainer, Roy Burkhardt.

"Oh, the knee isn't troubling me a bit," he said, "but why wait until something starts hurting? Unless somebody else has first call on the diathermy machine, Roy, I figure some heat wouldn't hurt the leg any." A writer moved in and asked him if that bat had really slipped out of his hands.

"You must be slipping, Eddie," Jim said, grinning. "I always thought you guys gave your opinion before you asked for one." The reedy voice of Del Stackpole, one of Strager's mound standbys, caught his attention. Stackpole lived out in Eloise, a small but refined suburb about ten miles outside the city. He was inviting Kershaw, Duke McIver, and a couple of other players to his home for a cookout. They could bring their wives or sweethearts. Jim knew that if he happened to be married to one of the Gabors he would not be able to crash that exclusive set—not a man who swallowed a handful of canapes at a time, and smelled of chewing tobacco!

The old resentments gnawed at him. He forgot about therapy when he saw Kershaw taking a sixty-second workout with hair tonic in front of his locker. "Why don't they grab you for TV, Ron?" he hollered. "Why can't you show the public you hate greasy kid stuff as much as Stackpole?"

The pitcher's eyes blazed. Stackpole snapped, "And why aren't you taking the part of the bum bathing with Dial soap in a rain barrel? Or would you still smell of scrap tobacco and other things?"

Jim replied through teeth almost shut, "If this club didn't need your right arm so bad I'd tear it off you and wrap it around your neck!"

Hank Bruda stepped in between the two players, Stan Jaciuk right behind him. "Bruckner," Bruda snapped, "You use a big needle. If you can't take the jabs, sew up your lip."

"Yeah, Hank." Jim drew a deep breath and gave the slugger a smile. He liked Bruda and wanted his respect. "Just let me get my foot out of my big mouth." He nudged Del Stackpole in the ribs. "Forget it, kid," he said, and moved toward his locker. He had barely finished dressing when Mike Strager sent for him.

Charlie Overman, waiting for him nearby, grinned wide. "Will it be Paducah or Oshkosh, Jim?"

When Jim walked in, Strager was sitting at the desk in his office chewing on a cigar that seemed to be halfway down his throat. The manager's slate blue eyes crackled under his bushy brows and his prominent jaw seemed twice its normal size.

"Want to see me, Mike?"

"No! But it's necessary, Bruckner. You turned loose a full-scale riot out there and you look as innocent as a choirboy. You're not going to turn this game into a Pier Six brawl, mister, and you remember that! If you're going by a certain book you'd better throw it away. Times have changed, Jim. This isn't a mug's game!"

"Mike, it's still a jungle and you know it. They'll get you if you don't get them first. That pitch could have spilled my brains out, even with the hard hat on. I'll play nice if the other guys play nice!" He sat down in a chair and stabbed a finger at the manager. "I've always had to do it the hard way. I don't know any other. My old man worked in a Chicago brewery and most every night he came home loaded with samples. There was only one way out of the cold water flat we laughingly called a home, and that was to beat my way out with a baseball bat. I played baseball every day, and at night, too, when the kids around Halstead and Alaska could find enough light from the street lamps."

Strager tossed his cigar away and gestured impatiently. "Stop, Bruckner, Or I'll bust out crying. Hundreds of kids had the same start. Now they're bankers and lawyers and——"

Jim got half out of his chair. "Not these kids coming up today, like Kershaw, Stackpole, Lorber, Loun and most of the others. They had the chance to play Little League and

20

American League ball. They went to college because a lot of big league clubs paid their way through. Me, Strager? Nobody, but nobody sponsored the kind of kids that came from my section of the town. They were beyond redemption by the time they were ten years old. I got lucky, like the old Babe. My old man keeled over one day, and my mother ran off and left me! They put me in a home, Mike, that had a baseball team."

He paused and Strager, still impatient, snapped, "Go on, get it off your chest."

"I got my start crashing a semi-pro game, with a team called the Englewood Grays. I told their manager his first baseman was a bum and I could play rings around him. I was seventeen. That manager said I could have a crack at the job if I could take it away from the guy who had it. I took it away, Mike, losing three teeth."

Strager lit a fresh cigar and peered at Jim for a long moment. "Oh, you're tough, Bruckner. You've been proving it ever since, using your roughhouse tactics to compensate for certain baseball talent you lack. I'm warning you. Bob Vick recommended we take you on because of your hitting, and you can't question the G.M. You let your bat do the talking from now on, Bruckner. If it gets too quiet, out you go."

"Fair enough," Jim said, "but you have to admit a guy has to play more than once or twice a week to stay sharp, Mike."

"I'll use you when and where I see fit," Strager said flatly, and dismissed Jim with a wave of his hand.

Charlie Overman was waiting for him outside. When they came out through the players' gate, some kids swarmed around them. Most of them were noisy, anything but shy and retiring. One teen-ager wearing tight black pants, pointed shoes and an air force windbreaker shoved a score card under Jim's nose. "Sign it, huh, Bruckner? Man, that was somethin'. I wish the bat had taken Ridel's head off."

"Your public," Overman said when they finally got to where

his old car was parked. "Know what one fresh brat asked me? Did I ever hit against Cy Young."

On the way to Detroit's north side, where they shared a small apartment, Overman admitted he was curious about Jim's conversation with Strager.

"Let's say Mike doesn't go for soap operas, Charlie. The meat end of his talk was 'or else,' if you get what I mean. What is it I'm supposed to have? Color? Well, Strager is color-blind. He's not making this club go all out, no holds barred. It's a wonder the Cougars aren't in the cellar."

"Maybe you've got it all wrong, Jim."

He gave Overman a sour look, but saved his breath, for the forty-year-old outfielder was one of those ballplayers who had put in almost fifteen years in the majors without creating much of an image. Just the adequate .270 hitting journeyman operator who had been with five clubs. He was quiet and unassuming, and would most likely spend the next ten years somewhere as a coach. He was the kind of player who would, after he'd hung up his spikes, be quickly forgotten by the fans.

The purely business side of baseball had risen, Jim Bruckner was certain, and nobody could tell him anything different. How many players, even the young squirts, were running out pop flies or a ball hit to the mound? There was margin for error in both instances. Yeah, there were the fringe benefits. This was a time when all the hustlers and crumb pickers were hovering like vultures on the edge of the game of baseball as they did in tin pan alley. Guys like Stackpole smelled out the side money, hiring an agent's nose at the standard price of ten per cent. Who did run a ball club's publicity kick?

Eating steaks in their favorite tavern, they heard a newscaster's comments on the afternoon game. ". . . It is anybody's guess whether or not Bruckner let the bat slip out of his hand after being dropped into the dirt by Ridel. Beyond a doubt, however, a real rhubarb took place, and when it

22

was over Bruckner drove in the winning runs with a scorching double down the left field line. A player stamped out of the Durocher-Hemus-Stanky mold, the veteran outfielder has captured the fancy of the Detroit fans. Bruckner has appeared in only twenty ball games, but he is hitting .291 and has driven in twelve runs. Out on the coast, the Pilgrims lead L.A., 4-2 at the end of the sixth. . . ."

Jim Bruckner drained a tall glass of iced coffee and felt very good indeed. Several of the customers at the surrounding tables became aware of his presence. One or two stopped at his table to congratulate him and wish him well. Had he ever been that street Arab back in Chicago, the toughest stick-ball player in his tough neighborhood?

Overman asked, "Who do we draw tomorrow night, Jim?"

"Bob Stratton for sure. I've never hit that guy too good. He has the best sinker in the business."

"Then you have some humility," Overman said, grinning.

"I'll look the word up, Charlie. I'll let you know."

2 ⚾

THE NEXT NIGHT MOVED IN, HOT AND HUMID. IT HAD RAINED most of the day, and the weathermen in the area promised thundershowers before midnight. The head groundkeeper advised that the tarpaulin be left on the infield until game time, and the players of both clubs welcomed the washout of the pre-game workouts. In the Detroit dressing room Jim pulled the elastic knee bandage in place, one ear cocked to catch some of the talk running through the big room. Wally Bream, the first base coach and a confirmed worrywart, said to Hank Bruda, "He's jugglin' the battin' order up again. Mike's in there outguessin' himself. That Stratton don't care who hits from which side, and I told him that."

Jim wondered if he'd get in there tonight. Jaciuk had only had two for fourteen in the last four ball games. He swung his head around and picked up Bream's glance. The coach read the question in his eyes. "I don't know, Jim. I don't think so."

"Maybe he's savin' me for the big series, Wally." He got up and reached into his locker for his uniform, and was pulling the lower half on when Strager came out of his office. The manager sought out Art DeLeon and told him he would be at second base for the windup game against New York, and then he moved on to where Jaciuk sat.

"You don't start, Stan," he said tersely.

Jim's head snapped up. He froze in the act of tieing a shoelace, and Strager came in close and asked, "How's your legs, Bruckner? Think you can last a few innings?"

"If my crutches don't break, Mike. If they'll let me hit from a wheelchair."

Strager's craggy face did not change expression. "You're in left," he snapped, and walked away.

There was a noticeable letdown in the horseplay, talk and laughter that usually filled the Cougar dressing room, mostly on the part of a few rookies and the old campaigners. The time for the big league clubs to get down to the player limit was rapidly approaching. The axe poised over several heads, and Jim knew his own could easily be in jeopardy. He let his eyes wander. They fell on Tex Loun, the third baseman, who was busily polishing the lenses of his eyeglasses, and an expression close to scorn crept into them. He had an aversion for eyeglasses. To him they suggested weakness, and he even wore sunglasses with reluctance. Not for a moment would he admit that this mental opposition stemmed from far back—the day he had lost his temper and punched a kid who had worn them. It had cost his father nearly thirty dollars, and Jake Bruckner had taken his son's brand new baseball glove and thrown it into the furnace as a result.

The muffled roar of the Briggs Stadium crowd seeped into the dressing room, the papers that morning having predicted another big gate. Jim reached to the top shelf of his locker for his package of scrap tobacco, and cramming a sizable amount of it into his right cheek, allowed a grin to bisect his face. The fans were pouring in, hoping that the feud would still be on. Strager, without doubt, aware of the profit that comes from giving the public what it wanted, had given him a starting role.

The big shirtsleeve crowd gave the Cougars a warm and thunderous welcome when they took over their dugout twenty minutes before game time. A loud voice just behind the dugout roof yelled at Strager, "You playin' Bruckner, Mike?"

26

"Yeah, we want Bruckner!"

Jim stayed out of sight, abstractedly watched Del Stackpole warm up with Irv Greenbaum, Strager's second-line backstop, and strove to ignore the rifle-crack sounds of the ball Stratton was throwing in a Titan catcher's big mitt. He kept wiping his hands dry against his knees, ever mindful of that soggy outfield, where a man could slip and injure a muscle, a bone, or a tendon. Sweat beads formed around his mouth as his fingers strayed over his bandaged knee. A doctor in Omaha had assured him that there was really nothing more to worry about. They had given his water-on-the-knee trouble a big name—called it a not too severe case of synovitis. He straightened the leg and then suddenly bent the knee, but felt no sign of a twinge.

"We'll need frog feet and snorkels out there," Hank Bruda said, when there were only a few minutes left. "What did you say, Art?" he asked DeLeon. "What does Stratton throw that's tough? Everythin' but the rosin bag. If you have the guts, crowd the plate on him, and you might get a walk."

The thousands clamored for things to get under way. They got on every Titan who showed his face ten feet out in front of their dugout. The big mouth back of the home bench kept at Strager. "You stalling for rain, Mike? Is it true you're gettin' fired?"

Jim Bruckner sighed with relief when the bell rang. Beyond the infield he splashed alongside Hank Bruda, and when the crowd occupying the left field stands spotted him, they loudly took him to their hearts. He turned a deaf ear to the accompanying barrage of verbal brickbats from the neutral fans and Titan sympathizers, and looked up into the artificial daylight when he took his playing position against the New York lead-off hitter, Riseman. The shortstop seldom hit to the opposite field.

Stackpole's first pitch brought the usual warmup roar on

the part of the crowd. It was a strike. Riseman let a wide one go by, then drilled the third pitch straight at Tex Loun on third, and the ball skipped through his legs and went into short right. Jim raced in, picked up the ball as the soggy turf slowed it down, and threw a strike to DeLeon at second; and DeLeon, seeing that the base runner had lost his footing putting on the brakes after a wide turn, whipped the ball to Russ Lorber at first. Riseman tried to scramble back but was a second too late. He got up and jawed at the umpire. Phipps, the Titan pilot, came out, and was ordered back in a hurry by the man in blue. The spectators screamed their delight over this hectic beginning, hoping that a bigger blaze would develop from this smoldering ember. Jim moved a little toward center when Lubec, the New York right fielder, came up to hit. Stackpole threw eight pitches before the hitter drove one to right center that Hank Bruda hauled in after a long run.

Parisi, with a batting average of .328, took a strike, fouled one back into the seats, then hung back and let Stackpole throw three pitches out of the strike zone. Jim heard Hank Bruda shout, "Back a little, Jim."

He was backtracking when Parisi got all of the good wood on a Stackpole pitch, and then he was running hard toward the barrier, glancing back over his shoulder to gauge the flight of the ball. He was on the running track when he sensed he had misjudged it, and wheeled back just in time to pick it off with his gloved hand a foot from the ground. The fans near the home dugout ribbed him when he came within earshot. Loudmouth yelled, "You should git a butterfly net, Bruckner. Every time a ball goes your way I shut my eyes an' say a prayer."

"As long as you catch 'em," Strager said when his left fielder dropped to the bench, and he slapped Loun on the rear. "Get us started, kid." Kershaw followed to the on-deck circle, and Jim went to the woodpile and selected his pet bat. Crouched on the dugout steps, he watched Stratton buzz two strikes right past Loun, and the third baseman looked bewildered as he moved out and asked Kershaw to throw him the pine tar rag.

"Stratton's as fast as I've ever seen him," Bert Alschul observed dryly. "We'd better be buntin' good tonight."

Loun struck out on three pitches, and Jim went out to the batter's circle and eyed Stratton closely as he worked on Kershaw. The Titan pitcher was always the master for five or six innings, but he seldom finished more than one game out of four. Tonight the humidity sucked the vital sap out of the toughest man, young, old, or in between. Kershaw swung at a ball shin high and walked away, and Jim strode to the plate, the fans coming fully alive. The Titan bench jockeys started their slander, and Riseman's reedy voice came out of the infield. "Wrap the showboat up, Bob. Curl it around his neck!"

Jim, standing deep in the batter's box, let a low pitch go by. The ball hit the plate and got a piece of Ricci's thumb before it hopped back to the stands. Ricci clamped his teeth over his meat-hand and Jim said, "I hope it's nothing trivial, Sam."

The Titan catcher seemed about to make an argument out of it when the New York trainer arrived. Ricci turned his back to the plate and let the first aid man spray his thumb with the freezing solution, and then the game was held up while Ricci fired a few practice throws. There was a smattering of applause for the New York catcher when he finally squatted down behind the plate.

Stratton came in with a slider that Jim elected to let go by, and the umpire's emphatic strike call whirled him around. "Cass, you missed that one," he snapped.

"Yeah? If I'd had that bat in my hand I wouldn't have, Bruckner!"

Ricci laughed through his mask as Jim dug in once more.

Stratton took a little off a curve ball and Jim swung too far out in front and fouled it back of third. He was certain now he'd get the fast ball. It hummed in, and he took a healthy cut and popped it high out into short right. Lubec, the Titan right-fielder, raced in. Kaula, the second baseman, ran out. Each fielder decided to let the other make the play. Both put on the brakes, and Jim, running out the high pop-up to the limit, raced for second when the ball dropped to the ground between them. Riseman got the throw-in from Kaula and put a vicious tag on Jim even though he knew the Cougar had made it with time to spare. Jim, knowing he would have a bruise on his shin for at least two days, got up slowly and banged the dirt off his uniform. "Four-eyes," he snapped at Riseman, "when I come back this way again, watch out!"

"Write me when you get to Oshkosh, Bruckner!"

Jim took his lead off second, yelling in at Hank Bruda to drive him home. The cleanup man cut at Stratton's first offering and slammed it through the middle, and Jim, on the move with the pitch, rounded third and came in to score. The Cougars needled him over the cheap hit, and Strager quieted them with his double-edged tongue. "That was real hustle," he snapped, "I wish it was catching, like typhoid." Jim took his place beside Charlie Overman, a small smile on his face. It was the first kind word he'd received from the manager since the opening of the season.

Watching Alschul hang in against the Titan pitcher, Jim felt a touch of misgiving. That pitch he'd popped up had looked as fat as a beachball coming in, but he had got only a small piece of the ball. Nine times out of ten he had pickled that kind of a pitch far out. He was up and yelling with the others when Alschul cracked a full-count pitch to right, but the ball curled foul at the last moment and brought a massed groan from the stands.

Jim settled back, idly watching Bob Stratton rub up a new ball. He told himself he had to shake himself of the mid-June jitters, forget the player cut, and get his hits. He had been up and down in this game like a bucket in a well. One more ticket

30

down and that would be it. He knew what he had to do, along with maintaining a respectable batting average. He had to keep stirring the fancy of the fans with his rock and sock type of play, keep them yelling his name and reminding the Detroit front office that their money kept the club in business. He must make sure he continued giving the writers the colorful copy that had been almost an unknown commodity since the Alley Gang passed into oblivion. He could not afford to give the opposition an inch. He had to keep knocking it down if it got in his way.

Kershaw, Loun, Lorber, and several others here in the dugout, he reflected, had seen only the front yard, the elegant façade of baseball. If it happened to be in the cards that they should be shunted to the back alleys of the minors where they had to show their claws to survive, they might perhaps think kindlier of old Jim Bruckner.

The crack of Alschul's bat snapped his head up, and the Titan center fielder, Brossett, ran back, whirled and caught the ball deep on the warning track. Jim went back out there, and with Brossett leading off for New York, moved with the shift Strager and most of the other managers in the league put on the slugger.

Stackpole tried to keep the ball low and outside, and missed with his first two pitches. Brossett rocketed his let-up curve over the roof, foul, then watched two go by outside for a walk. Sam Ricci stepped in and whacked Stackpole's first pitch between right and center; and Jim was legging it after the lofty fly when Hank Bruda shouted him off. Hank gathered it in, and Jim called out, "Thanks, Hank. They don't pay me for fielding."

The center fielder shot back, "Forget it. I'll be old myself some day."

Brossett, respecting Bruda's arm, only faked an advance to second.

Fullbright, the Titan third baseman, a spray hitter, worked

Stackpole to the limit, then began fouling off pitches he figured Cass Byron might call either way. Stackpole buzzed his fast ball over and Fullbright slammed it through the hole at short, sending Brossett to second. Strager came to the top step of the dugout and waved to the bullpen, the early SOS putting a blaze into the Cougar pitcher's eyes. He threw a slider that nipped the outside corner, got his fast ball by Tillotson, the New York right fielder, for a second strike, then gave the hitter a full effort but yanked back on the string. The batter let the ball float across his chest, letter high, then fired his bat away. Jim ran in from left with Bruda.

Jeremiah Jones, first up for Detroit in the bottom of the second, immediately stepped out of the batter's box when loud-mouth, back of the home dugout, yelled, "Stand in there, Jer'. Don't let them disintegrate you, man!"

Half a thousand fans in the immediate vicinity quickly assured the smart aleck that they would personally remove him from the scene and heave him down the nearest ramp if he dared to make a similar remark just once more. Jim came out of the dugout with half a dozen other angry Cougars and had no trouble picking out the man in the gaudy yellow and green sports shirt. "Knock it off, you chowderhead!" he shouted, "or I'll climb up there and shove my arm down your throat."

Strager grabbed Jim's arm. "All right, knock it off, Bruckner. The fans know you're here!"

Sam Ricci, the Titan catcher, growled through his mask, "The cops should throw that guy out now. Bruckner doesn't need no help starting a riot."

Stratton began to work on the dusky Detroit outfielder, feeding him breaking stuff. The count against him, three and one, he fired a fast ball, and Jones swung and rattled it against the barrier in right for two bases. The fans came up, clamoring for a big inning. A lot of them booed when Strager's first base-man, Lorber, dug in against Stratton. Playing his second season for the Cougars, the big youngster was in a woeful batting slump.

Jim watched Lorber's feet as the man swung at two pitches and missed. The power turned loose in a bat comes from the weight of the body as it changes from the rear foot to the one facing the pitcher. Lorber was not sliding his front foot forward in taking his cut. His movement was almost a high step. More than once the past few days he'd wanted to tell Lorber about this, but he was ever aware of the fact that advice was the last thing Strager and the rest of the players wanted or expected from him.

Lorber looked at a third strike, made his way to the dugout, head bent against the big crowd's boos. Art DeLeon moved in, and Stratton brushed him back as he crowded the plate. The Cougar second baseman, a little shaken up by the fast ball that came within an inch of his chin, kept his distance and finally popped out to the Titan shortstop. Stackpole, one scratch hit to his credit all season, struck out on four pitched balls.

The Cougars made their one-run lead stand up through five innings, but Brossett, with one man out in the top of the sixth, got hold of the pitch he liked and put it far beyond the reach of the Detroit outfielders, into the stands in right. Sam Ricci reached second when Jim bobbled his line single into left center, and a shrill voice suggested that he get himself a peach basket. When Jim faded back to his position, an empty beverage can sailed past him. Time was called as he retrieved it, and then a roar went up when he fired it back.

Fullbright worked Stackpole to an even count, then slashed a hit into right that brought Ricci around with the lead run. Strager made his way to the mound in long strides, and Alschul, Kershaw, and Lorber joined the summit meeting. Stackpole was allowed to stay in, knowing his fate if he lost the next hitter, Tillotson.

The Titan left fielder fouled off the first pitch, let a high pitch alone, then drove a high fly to left. Jim ran in a few steps, ran back, circled under the ball, and finally hauled it in. The fans gave him a backhanded cheer, and he turned his face up at them and squirted tobacco juice through his teeth.

Stackpole got Kaula, the Titan keystone man, to foul out to Alschul, and when Jim reached the dugout, Strager turned his gamiest vocabulary against him. "I've got a good mind to plaster you with a fifty buck fine, Bruckner! Maybe you'll get worse from the league president. You could have hit somebody with that tin can, and the club would maybe have a law suit on its hands."

"And if somebody skulls me, the club will give them a season pass," Jim snapped back.

"I'm for that!" Strager roared.

With Loun leading off, Jim pulled a bat from the rack, ready to take over the on-deck circle behind Kershaw. Loun singled off the Titan first baseman's shin, and the rookie shortstop, Kershaw, swung at Stratton's third offering and sent the Titan's Kaula into short right to spear his ground ball. Kershaw was thrown out by a step, but no play could be made on Loun.

"The crowd-pleasin' comedian," Ricci said when Jim stepped in. "A leaky showboat."

"What do the Titan bosses feed you when the bananas give out, Sam?" Jim scooped up some dirt and scrubbed the bat handle clean of moisture. "And what's happened to your cheap Chinese home runs?"

"Get in there and play ball," Cass Byron said.

Jim stared out at Stratton and saw signs that the heat was telling on the New York pitcher. A little war of nerves here, he decided, might speed the flinger to the showers. When Stratton got set to throw, Jim stepped out, exploring his right eye with an index finger. He blinked the eye at Cass Byron, finally said, "Okay," and stepped back in. He took a called

34

strike, rocked back from an inside pitch, and then asked the umpire to examine the ball. Stratton angrily threw it in to Ricci. Jim said, "Check it, Cass. Tell Stratton to dry his fingers."

The umpire examined the ball, gave Jim a threatening look, and threw it back to the mound. The fans were relishing the Bruckner antics to the full, and they let him know it loud and clear. Jim took a foothold, then went sprawling into the dirt when the duster nicked the visor of his hard hat and sent it spinning from his head. Jim loped to first base, Cass Byron strode halfway to the mound and gave Stratton a stern warning, and then Phipps stormed out of the Titan dugout, his neck fiery red. Mike Strager raced to the diamond, and Briggs Stadium was in an uproar.

3 ⊜

THE MANAGERS ORDERED BACK TO THEIR RESPECTIVE DUG-
outs, the game got under way once more. With one out and
Hank Bruda hitting, Jim edged off first. He hoped to get a
head start, in case Hank hit the ball on the ground, and pre-
vent a possible double play. Stratton fired over, keeping him
tight. Jim needled Parisi, the veteran Titan first baseman.
"You should lay off the spaghetti. You're getting a real pot."

"Big mouth," Parisi fired back. "You're a real phony, Bruckner."

Jim took his lead when Stratton turned the ball loose. Bruda
slammed it to deep short and Riseman dug it out and flipped
it to Kaula, covering second. Just as the infielder pivoted,
Jim barreled in and knocked him off his feet, dumping Kaula
halfway to the outfield grass. Bruda was safe on the fielder's
choice. Loun reaching third. Jim, on his way to the dugout,
held up and glanced over his shoulder. Kaula was not getting
up, and Titan players were gathering around him. "Better get
under cover, Bruckner," the Titan pitcher threatened.

The New York manager came out with the Titan trainer.
Kaula was sitting up when Jim reached the bench. The Cougars were as quiet as the stands were noisy. Stan Jaciuk gave
Jim a hard look. "You never pull a punch, do you? You never
think you might cripple a man and take the bread and butter
out of his family's mouth."

"A buck will get you ten they don't find spike marks in him," Jim said. "Since when has breaking up a double play become illegal?" He glanced toward Strager, but the man had his back turned, busy with the signals he was relaying to the third base coach.

Kaula got to his feet and walked around, and the crowd gave him some applause. Stratton, his inner defense set once more, began to work carefully on Bert Alschul. He got behind three and nothing, and activity broke loose in the visitors' bullpen. He got an automatic strike across, then fired a half speed curve. The big Cougar catcher timed it right and rode the ball to deep right, a foot inside the foul line. Tillotson, the Titan fielder, played it off the wall to perfection, and turned loose a throw that held Bruda on third, allowing only one run to score. Jeremiah Jones, however, brought Hank in with a clean shot through the middle, and Detroit was ahead, 3-2.

Strager, while Phipps went out to bring in a new pitcher, called Ken Lorber back from the on-deck circle and picked up Charlie Overman with his eyes. Overman, as it turned out, had no turn at bat, for the New York relief man induced DeLeon to roll weakly to the box.

With a one-run lead, Strager juggled his defensive lineup, putting Jaciuk in left, and giving Jim the first baseman's mitt. He replaced DeLeon at second with Zach Jones. Stackpole held on by virtue of great support until the top of the eighth when the New York pilot sent a pinch hitter in to hit for Stratton. The man bunted the first pitch just inside the third base line, and Loun raced in, bare-handed the ball and fired to first. The throw was short, pulling Jim off the bag, and the Titans had something going.

Titan thunder and lightning struck. Lubec doubled, and Parisi homered. Stackpole gave way to Lenny Dee, who received a brief ovation when he struck out the dangerous Brossett. Ricci, the New York catcher, silenced the crowd again when he planted the second pitch thrown to him in the bleachers. Dee went out, and Pedro Camacho came in to get the side out after allowing two more Titans to get on.

The Cougars could do nothing with the Titan relief pitcher the rest of the way, Jim registering the final out with three futile swings. Tempers were stretched thin when the players reached the clubhouse. "We lost it, six-three," Bert Alschul growled as he peeled off the catching gear, known as the tools of ignorance to ballplayers everywhere. "But the crowd got their money's worth. They got the Bruckner sideshow." He glared at Jim. "Why don't you throw a punch with your bat when we need it? You looked like an old woman swatting flies durin' that last strikeout."

"You're one of the big money men," Jim countered. "You didn't earn a buck and a half tonight." He pulled off his soggy uniform and dumped it into a big hamper.

Kershaw, eyeing the old scars on his legs, remarked, "He who lives by the sword—" and Charlie Overman suggested that the rookie had ten more years to serve before he had a right to judge his elders in the profession.

The showers cooled the Cougars off a little. They turned their thoughts to the three game series coming up with the Boston Pilgrims, hoping to make up lost ground against the seventh place club. Following that set, they were scheduled to hop a plane to Los Angeles, where they would begin a seventeen game road trip—that is, those players who would survive the dangling front office axe.

Overman, dressing next to Jim, was resigned to his fate. "That Harvard professor said it all once, Jim: 'Success is but a fortuitous combination of circumstances.' Suppose I'd had a chance to pinch hit tonight and belted one all the way, and turned that game right around? That would have been a reprieve."

The noise of the traffic outside the stadium turned Jim's

thoughts to the Detroit fans. He had been giving them the excitement and the laughs they craved. They thoroughly enjoyed both cheering and booing him. He was, it seemed, as dear to their hearts as had been Babe Herman to the Brooklyn fans of long ago. He was the crowd pleaser. He made the turnstiles click. No one could convince him at that moment that the Cougars were even thinking of letting him go.

When they returned from breakfast next morning, Jim settled down with a Detroit morning newspaper, turned to the sports page, and scanned a daily column labeled "Sportsides." His name leaped out at him. "Bruckner," Harry Nabors had written, "was possibly born thirty years too late. There are many fans who do not fully appreciate his antics and swashbuckling tactics, his continued baiting of opposing players, or the way he throws his spikes around. True, he came up the hard way, the hungriest of ballplayers, and perhaps he's trying too hard to meet the trials of a world he never understood. He does 'play for the crowd.' There's something of the ham in the veteran . . ."

Jim threw the paper aside, and Charlie Overman glanced up from a letter he had received in the morning mail. "Nabors hit you again?" he asked.

"I'll take that guy apart yet," Jim snapped. "He's got himself a head doctor's diploma?" The wide grin on Overman's sun-baked face shook him up. "It's not funny, Charlie. If you——"

"Excuse me if I look a little happy, Jim." He waved the letter at his roommate. "A few days ago, figuring I've had it, I dropped a line to Gus Vogel. We played together on the Kansas City Blues six or seven years ago."

"Sure, Vogel was a third baseman. One of the best," Jim said.

"Gus has a good thing going for him in Elm Grove, North Carolina," Overman said. "A baseball camp for boys eight to eighteen. He wants me there in time for the July sessions. So I will welcome my unconditional release."

"Man, the kids have it easy today, Charlie. Everything made to order for baseball talent." He kicked a hassock across the room. "If those kids only knew how I had to——"

"Oh, knock it off, Jim," Overman said angrily. "Cut your chains loose. These kids today have to pay for that training. Most of them earn the money."

"If they'd had the camps in the old days," Jim griped, "I'd have got to one of them, even if I'd had to steal the dough."

"That I believe," Overman said. "Sit down and let me give it to you straight. Up to now I've kept my lip buttoned because I had to live with you. If you had really tried to improve yourself the past ten years, both on and off the diamond, you would not be sweating out a player cut. To be brutally frank, you're capitalizing on being a mug. You're the punchy prizefighter sticking out his chin to hear the crowd roar."

Jim started to get up and Overman waved him back. "When I'm finished you can take a poke at me if you wish, Jim. You know what I actually believe? You're a much better gloveman than you pretend to be. No doubt, somewhere back, a writer mentioned that you were a riot circling under a flyball and that the fans had delighted in your clumsiness. They created the image and you grabbed at it. The writers have kept you on top, Jim. They established you as a character instead of a top-notch ballplayer. You're that copy they dream about. As far as your public is concerned, you're an extinct biped from a lost world. They pay their money to revel in the difference between the rough and tumble past and the genteel present. You don't believe they haven't seen hundreds of .280 hitters before?"

"You've had your say?" Jim asked, his jaw muscles tightening, his eyes telling Overman to be ready to throw his guard up. Suddenly he let his breath sough out and managed a crooked grin. "You lost me halfway through that sermon, preacher. Shall I take up the collection?"

"That reminds me," Overman said. "That book you go by. Throw it away. I read a couple of chapters in it a few days ago, and I'll still take Goldilocks and the three bears." He reached for a jacket draped over the back of a chair. "Jim, you could be a likable cuss if you tried. See you later. I'm going out and send Gus a wire."

When Overman left, Jim felt that he had to go to the book *Me and the Alley Gang,* by Roaring Terry Flynn. He could not afford to allow one small chink in his armor. Flynn, the man who had played third base for that St. Louis club, wrote, "A man had to be able to take it in those days, even to win a place in the batting cage before the game. They held as a common enemy any rookie who tried to break in. They battled off the playing field, a rough and ready lot as a whole. If one was caught fraternizing with the enemy on or off the field he had to face a kangaroo court in the clubhouse.

"They hit at a ball much less lively than the ones used today, and no new ball was put in play every time it picked up a little grass stain or a speck of dirt. Some of the gloves used by the present-day crop are like baskets. Why, this new breed even wear shin-guards at the plate. The old Alley Gang represented the pure dream of the game of baseball for its own sake. Now it is a livelihood, just a business with all the refinements enjoyed by big business executives, together with comparable salaries and bonuses. . . ."

Jim was putting the book back on a shelf when Overman returned. The old pro asked sourly, "It gave you a lift?"

"You think that Flynn spread it on thick, Charlie? Compared with what I went through, he and that bunch rode a red carpet. I played my first game for pay in a league where two hundred people was an overflow crowd. It was in the Blue Ridge, Charlie, and half the fans couldn't read what the letters said on the front of our shirts. I got three hits the first game I played, and a week later my average was .374. What happened? One day I walked into my room in the flea-trap they called a hotel and found both my bats broken in half. A big brute who had been benched because of me owned up to it. I waded into him, and he half killed me."

Overman nodded, "I can believe it. You didn't by any chance throw the weight of that batting average around? And your own weight, Jim?"

"Meaning what, Charlie?"

"The look you usually wear on your face invites trouble. I doubt if you change it often. But you'd better forget the past. This is the space age, and ballplayers like Terry Flynn have gone out along with hoop skirts and mens' elastic garters."

Jim sat on the bench that night when Tom Ogden, Strager's left-hander, fired his first pitch in at the Boston leadoff man, Kittredge. Before the game, while he was taking his swings in the batting cage, a lot of his old teammates had soundly razzed him. He could expect even worse if Strager saw fit to send him in there for the late innings. As Kittredge fouled off Ogden's second pitch, Jim's mind brushed back over the days he'd spent in the Massachusetts city noted for its culture. A grin twisted his face, making the bulge in his right cheek jump. Man, what the fans there had said to him! They'd used a vocabulary saltier than the codfish they ate. Apparently, he mused, the elite of Boston never came to Fenway.

Kittredge grounded out to Zach Jones, at second for the Cougars, and Ogden peered in at the Pilgrim first baseman, Toucette, currently hitting .298. He shook off Alschul's sign once, twice; then he nodded and went into a full windup. Toucette stepped up to meet the fast ball and drove it over Jaciuk's head in deep left. The ball bounced off the barrier, and Toucette reached second standing up. The fans began to squirm in their seats, and a lot of their racket tapered off. The

Boston one-two punch, Nick Lomski at the plate, Dino Vita in the on-deck station, prompted a brief conference on the part of Strager's battery.

"What's the problem, Ogden?" a fan yelled from behind first, "Walk him and then pick him off!"

Ogden kept two pitches low and outside to the left-handed pull-hitter. They both missed the plate, and Strager went to the lip of the dugout and crouched there. He waved Hank Bruda back in center. Lomski swung at a slider and fouled it outside third, nearly skulling the Pilgrim traffic man working there.

Jim Bruckner allowed it was about time to work on Lomski himself. He knew the big outfielder well. A man with a hair-trigger temper, he was often susceptible to rough riding from bench. Jim cupped his hands over his mouth and shouted, "Hey, Nick, how's your brother-in-law?"

Lomski stepped out, ostensibly to get dirt on his hands, but Jim read the irritation in Lomski's eyes when the hitter glared at him. "If there's anything Nick hates," he said to the Cougar bench, "It's his wife's brother. The guy moved in the day his sister got married and hasn't worked a day since."

Jim kept working the spurs. "Hey, Nick! He still uses your razor? Drives your car?"

Lomski swung viciously at a curve around his shoulders and struck out. Before he turned toward his dugout he seemed on the verge of hurling his bat at the Detroit bench.

"I'll take an assist," Jim said, laughing deep in his throat.

"It beats me how you've lived so long," Arturo DeLeon said, his voice edged. "Sure, ribbing the other people is part of the game, Bruckner, but when you do it, I feel somehow that it should be considered against the rules."

Strager flung over his shoulder, "I'll buy that."

"I love you all, too," Jim ground out.

Dino Vita was anything but thin-skinned, and the Pilgrim cleanup hitter was built like Plymouth Rock above the waist. If he had a weakness at the plate it was at the one in the dining room. Vita was hitting .341 and he had clubbed nine home runs.

Tom Ogden took a lot off his fast ball, electing to let Vita use his own power if he nailed one to his liking. With two out, he gave the slugger nothing too good to swing at, but with the count even at two balls and two strikes, Vita, always hit-hungry, swung at a pitch below his knees and golfed it into the stands in left.

Ogden, rattled from head to foot by the long ball, walked the next Boston batter, and only a great catch by Jeremiah Jones in right saved him from an early shower.

The Cougars only nibbled at the Boston right-hander's hurling for five innings, and got a base runner only as far as second. Strager's mood got saw-toothed; and in the sixth, with Hank Bruda on first, one out, and the Cougars three runs behind, he called Lorber back and told Jim to reach for a bat. The crowd responded to the strategy fullheartedly. They always welcomed the stormy petrel. When Jim dug in, Wilmot, the Boston catcher, perhaps even more abusive to hitters than Sam Ricci of the Titans, plied his big needle.

"You still got that housemaid's knee, Jim?"

Jim sprayed Wilmot's shoes with tobacco juice, swung his head around and waggled his bat at Al Grover. Grover's fast ball hummed in and he let it go by. It was a strike. Wilmot said through his mask, "I heard you challenged that Cassius Clay to a popoff contest, Bruck. You'll win easy."

Jim grinned, picked up a handful of dirt, checked the direction of the wind by the flags, and threw it away. Some of it got into Wilmot's eyes, and the backstop whipped off his mask and called time. "Sorry, Frank," he said, and the fans were buzzing, sensing a break in the monotony. The umpire cautioned Jim, and the Pilgrim manager, Ossie Jameson, hurried to the plate to see what was boiling.

"How's things, Ossie?" Jim asked with exaggerated politeness when the Hub pilot turned to go back.

"Great, now you're not with us, Bruckner," Jameson fired back, and the man in blue ordered the action to continue.

Grover threw a sinker that Jim missed by a foot, and Frank Wilmot walked out in front of the plate to throw the ball back. "Another one, Al. A sinker for a stinker."

"Hold it down," the umpire said, sniffing storm clouds.

A curve came in, and Jim cut hard and drove it high over the infield, the Pilgrim shortstop taking it after waving the third baseman off. Jim, after running it out all the way, returned to the dugout in time to hear Ogden grumbling down his rain barrel. "The last three games I've worked, I've pitched my brains out, and you drumsticks have given me just two runs. Don't you like me?"

Jeremiah Jones's bat made that certain sound like a rifle-crack just as the pitcher got the last two words out of his mouth, and the crowd came up in full voice. The Boston right fielder waved goodbye to the ball as it sailed into the seats. Crossing the plate, Jeremiah slapped his smaller brother, Zach, waiting to hit, on the stern, as if to say, "You keep it goin', man."

Zach Jones singled, and then Strager had to consider deeply. His pitcher was due up, and he had been going along well the last two innings. Just as the umpire began to get restless, he called Ogden back, stabbed a finger at Irv Greenbaum, a first-year man up from Class AA. Greenbaum, after running out the string, looked at a third strike, and Mike Strager picked up a soiled towel and slammed it down again. His temper cooled a few moments later when Wilmot wild-pitched to Loun, sending Zach Jones to second.

Loun, a banjo hitter, got the green light on a three and one pitch, and blooped it out to short left; and Zach, running on the two out situation, came in with the second run for Detroit. Boston's pilot, Jameson, considered Grover had gone as far as he dared let him, and walked to the mound. The relief pitcher, Embree, finally got to work and induced Kershaw to ground out, short to first.

The Cougars were blanked the rest of the way. Jim came up in the eighth and rolled to the pitcher, and felt the sting of the crowd and the taunts from the Pilgrim bench. In the ninth he nearly set up another Boston run when he dropped a throw from second that meant a possible double play. He never remembered a more miserable night, not even as a kid when he'd been kept overnight in detention.

4 ⚾

AT BREAKFAST THE NEXT MORNING, CHARLIE OVERMAN AGREED
that Jim had had a bad night. "You'll get those kind of days,
too. It's what you do in between that makes or breaks you." He
rattled the newspaper he was reading. He folded it to a certain
page and handed it over to Jim.

The quote was in Nabors' column: " 'It was no accident,'
the Boston catcher told the writers in the visitors' dressing room.
'Bruckner threw that dirt in my eyes deliberately. They ought
to throw him out of baseball.' "

"I don't think even your public thought that was funny,"
Overman remarked. "The kids read sports columns. It isn't
setting them much of an example."

"I don't remember any youth guidance character ever bother-
ing about me," Jim replied angrily. "Let them look after themselves."

Overman clamped a hand to his head. "Oh, brother, you are
a hard case. Everything bad that's happened to you must happen to everybody else; is that right? Or you won't be happy."

"Just do me a favor, Charlie. Get off my back."

"With pleasure, Jim. It's getting rough, riding a mule." He
waved his napkin. "Cease firing?"

Jim managed a small grin. Overman asked, "Who do you
think will be turned loose? Besides me, of course."

"Lorber, Udane, and that pitcher, Red Kraft."

Overman shook his head. "I don't know. That Lorber is a good glove man. Right now he's pressing a little hard, but who gives up quick on a guy who hit .301 last year? As a freshman."

"Second-year jinxes are tough to shake," Jim said. "I found that out in Cleveland."

Charlie Overman lit a cigar and eyed Jim while the outfielder's attention was drawn to the printed page. Here was a man who never touched tobacco in any form off the baseball diamond. The scrap, then, that Bruckner crammed into his cheek before a game, Overman was certain, was just another prop to make him look tougher than he really was. At the right time and place, he hoped, Jim might be convinced that in baseball as well as everyday living, facts and ideas that were right yesterday may be irrelevant or completely wrong today. Here was a man who had been slapped down as a kid, and he had been struggling to find ways of winning attention and significance ever since.

An hour after they reached their apartment, Overman got a long distance call from Gus Vogel, who wanted to know if Charlie could report to his baseball camp in about a week's time. "Gus," Jim heard Charlie say, "All Hades and high water won't stop me."

"I suppose you'll show the kids how to use a knife and fork correctly and make them brush their teeth, and tuck them in at night," Jim observed after Overman cradled the phone.

"Any job that has to do with youngsters involves some character building," Overman replied sharply. "Let me tell you something, Jim. More than eighty per cent of the old time pro ballplayers never saw a college, let alone high school. If the men who deliberately threw the 1919 Series had been of the caliber of the players today, there never would have been a baseball scandal. The biggest star on those Black Sox couldn't read or write."

50

Jim gestured with impatience. "The only reason a lot of ball-players today stay honest is because they make as much dough as bank presidents. I'll bet Brossett on the Titans gets more loot a year than they paid that whole Black Sox team. You ever play ball for fifty bucks a week, wash your own underwear and socks, and pay room and board when you weren't on the road? That's what I got with Rocky Point in the Blue Ridge. The kids today are born with golden spikes in their shoes."

"Your thinking is all wrong, Jim. It's too bad, I'll admit, that you started out with one foot in your mouth. But it's never too late to mend."

"Save your criticism for the small fry, Charlie." With an aggravating grin on one side of his mouth, Jim suggested that they go for a walk.

"Why not?" Overman replied. "I get little exercise gathering calluses on the Detroit bench."

They walked for about six blocks, then cut across a big play-ground where a bunch of kids were using the baseball diamond, but at the moment most of the players were milling around third base, their adolescent voices high-pitched. "Let's take a look," Jim said, and strolled in closer.

A big man wearing Chino pants, a baseball cap and Michi-gan Tech sweatshirt was helping a kid up from the dirt. The youngster's fingers were digging into his ribs, and tears ran down his cheeks. A redheaded boy was handing him a pair of glasses and saying, "Aw, come ah-h-hn, Vinnie. They ain't busted. And you only got some wind knocked out."

The big leaguers stopped on the skin-edge of the infield and watched the man with the college sweatshirt single out a husky teen-ager wearing only scuffed sneakers and faded blue jeans. His lecture was stern, a reminder that this was a playground and not a setting for a rumble. "If you can't play this game clean, Harvey, you'd better stay away in the future!"

"Look, Mr. Rossman, I read where Jim Bruckner of the

51

Cougars said the base path belongs to the runner," the boy on the carpet protested. "You have to———"

"We don't teach Bruckner's brand of baseball here, Harvey!" Rossman said, and Jim, his jaw muscles tightening, moved in.

Charlie Overman said, "Hold it, Jim."

The boys suddenly aware of visitors, broke apart. Jim strode up to Rossman, a small grin on his face. "You must be the supervisor here," he said. "I'm Jim Bruckner. This is Charlie Overman. What happened here?"

Rossman, a trace of embarrassment as well as surprise on his face, held out his hand. "Well, this is a surprise, and a great treat for the kids."

Jim appraised the boy who was wiping his face clean with the back of a hand. Less than a hundred and ten pounds soaking wet, he judged. His eyeglasses reminded him of a hooty owl he'd once seen.

"One of the boys came at Vinnie a little too hard," Rossman explained. "He didn't get out of the way in time."

The boys could not speak for the moment. They stared at the big leaguers as if they had just landed from Mars.

Jim said to the bespectacled kid, "You've got to be ready when they barrel in on you, especially if you wear those cheaters." He swung his eyes toward Rossman. "Don't you teach them the facts of life?"

Rossman's neck reddened. "If you mean the way you play it, Bruckner, no!"

Charlie said under his breath, "Okay, Jim, let's go and mind our own business."

The awe-stricken silence broke, and the boys surrounded the Detroit players, firing questions and asking for autographs. Rossman yelled, "Okay, fellers, one at a time!"

When they finally got loose and were near the street, Jim growled, "That college boy should teach ping-pong."

"Rossman . . . Rossman," Overman repeated. "Sure; now I remember. He's that guy six major league clubs want to ink. He led all intercollegiate players in hitting last spring with an average of .398."

"No kidding? What's Kershaw and Lorber hitting for us right now? Didn't they hit over .350 on the campus, Charlie?" Jim's eyes became a little hot. "That rah-rah boy—trying to make me look like a mug in front of those kids. . . . I sure was tempted to clobber him."

"No comment," Overman said under his breath.

The Cougar dressing room lacked much of the usual talk, griping and horseplay when the players suited up for the afternoon game. Four of their number would be among the missing when the plane took off for the coast on Sunday morning. If Mike Strager already knew the names of the victims, he gave no outward signs of such knowledge, but when he told Jim Bruckner he was to play first base instead of Lorber, many eyebrows lifted and surreptitious nods were exchanged. Jim felt a great lift as he reached for his sack of scrap tobacco. He guessed the front office knew where the bread of a sixth-place club was buttered. He turned toward Jeremiah Jones. "Remind me to get those airsick pills before we take off Monday, Jer'."

"Why don't you get yourself hypnotized 'fore the trip, Jim? Save you money, man."

Overman said close to Jim's ear, "Kershaw is sure running scared. Mike dropped him from number two to seven in the batting order. Ed Stangaard is either going to have the greatest or worst support of his career behind him today. Some might try too hard; some may figure 'So what?' "

"Yeah, even DeLeon has been talkin' mostly in Spanish, Charlie. The jitters are sure going out there with us."

Jim bent over and tightened his shoelaces, feeling a little nervousness himself. He would be hitting in the number two spot, where a hitter was expected to deliver. And the Pilgrims were throwing one of their best against the Cougars this afternoon, Fireball Earl Clough. Jim had to admit he'd never hit the guy very well—only around .250, give or take a couple of points. Clough wore glasses and could turn hog wild at any moment. Few hitters crowded the plate on him. The last time Jeremiah Jones had hit against him, the colored outfielder had said, "The man locates that plate by Braille."

A half hour later, taking over at first base, Jim wished he had been put in left field. The Pilgrim bench had him within earshot and lost no time badgering him. In the most remote seats in the stadium the fans could see his jaws wagging back at them and they saw in his scornful gestures the promise of an exciting afternoon.

Ed Stangaard retired the first two Boston hitters, Kittredge and Toucette, and then threw Lomski a curve that hung, and it was rapped to the right field corner for two bases. Dino Vita, after working the count on the Cougar left-hander even, slammed a pitch to deep short, and Kershaw dug out the ball and fired a low throw to first that skipped by Jim and rolled to the stands. Lomski came in to score, and Vita, not too fast a runner, pulled up at second. A big E went up on the board for Kershaw, but the Boston bench booed it. "Hey, Bruck!" a jockey shouted, "My grandmother could have come up with that throw!"

Stangaard struck out the visitors' number five hitter, and the big afternoon crowd noisily tuned up. Jim followed Tex Loun out of the dugout and knelt in the on-deck circle, and the customers back of the screen worked on him good-naturedly, trying to get his attention. He grinned into the dirt, hoping certain Detroit front office execs were listening.

His head snapped up when Clough's first pitch sent Loun staggering backward, and then Wilmot, the Pilgrim catcher, ripped off his mask when the umpire waved the Cougar leadoff man to first. Ossie Jameson, the Boston pilot stormed out of

54

the dugout, and Clough came running in from the mound. Jim strolled toward the plate and propped himself up by the handle of his bat. "I saw it," he called out. "It brushed Tex's sleeve."

"Keep out of this, Bruckner!" Cass Byron, the plate umpire, threw over his shoulder, then spun his head around and put his jaw close to Jameson's. Wilmot angrily snatched up his mask when the umpire gave his last warning, and Briggs Stadium was already in an uproar. The plate area finally cleared, Jim stepped in to face Clough. The erratic fireballer peered in for the sign, chewing furiously on a wad of gum. He nodded, and then cut loose with a curve that had Jim skipping rope.

The Cougar first baseman stepped out and looked at Cass Byron. "Take the plate out an' show it to him, will you?"

Half of the Boston infield came to the mound to steady their pitcher down. When Jim dug in again, he watched a blazing fast ball in the groove go by. He swung at the one and one pitch and hit into a fast double play, making an attempt to forestall it by sliding hard into the first-base bag. The crowd roared when Toucette was spilled just after taking the throw from second. When Jim reached the dugout, Strager snapped, "You even grandstand an out, don't you?"

"Let's say I try all the time, Mike," Jim said, giving the manager look for look.

Stan Jaciuk went down swinging at Clough's fireballs, and the Cougars took the field again. Stangaard's defense suddenly fell apart after he had retired the first Pilgrim hitter. Loun fielded a bunt nicely, then threw it high over Jim's head. Zach Jones bobbled a ground ball; and with two men on, Stremski, the Boston third baseman, blooped one into short left to score the second run for the visitors. Strager signaled for activity in his bullpen as Stangaard began working on the opposing pitcher. He struck Clough out, but Kittredge, beginning the Pilgrim hitting go-round once more, singled the third Boston run home. Mike Strager hurried to the mound, waving to the bullpen, the fans booing and peeling the Cougars of what dignity they possessed. A series sweep by the beantowners would drop Detroit to seventh.

The veteran relief man, Pedro Camacho, finished his warmup pitches and began working on Toucette. He got a strike across, gave the Pilgrim first baseman a big motion and yanked back on the string. Toucette swung and hit it into the right field stands to make the score 5-0, Boston. Nick Lomski ended the agony by flying out deep to Hank Bruda.

The mood of the fans and the Detroit bench got more ragged as the game progressed. Not until the sixth did the Cougars break through on Clough. A streak of wildness put McIver, hitting for Pedro Camacho, on. The Pilgrim pitcher hit Tex Loun for the second time; and Jim, wincing a little when the crowd got on him, sliced a hit into right that scored McIver. The RBI brought only cursory reaction from the fans. They seemed to have forgotten he was there. Toucette moved in to hold him on. The big first baseman growled, "Don't get smart again, Bruckner."

"Don't give me ideas, Harry." He took his lead, and jumped back when Clough threw over and bumped into Toucette, nearly shaking the ball loose from the Pilgrim's mitt.

"I said watch it, you showboat!" Toucette barked, and the fans became alive.

Jim kept worrying Clough as the pitcher worked on Jaciuk. When the Detroit fielder swung and missed for a second strike, Wilmot fired a bullet to Toucette, and Jim came back into the bag head first. Toucette brought the ball down hard against the top of his head, and for a moment he counted stars. "Try that on for size," Toucette said, and then Jim scrambled to his feet and made for the first baseman. Strager's coach quickly stepped in between, and players came off both benches.

The first base umpire warned Toucette. Behind the plate, Cass Byron made it plain to both managers that they were not

56

to take another step toward the diamond, and the flare-up died.

Jaciuk popped out to short, but Hank Bruda got all his power into one of Clough's fireballs and hit it into the seats in deep left, scoring behind Loun and Jim. Ossie Jameson came out and yanked Clough, and the fans took the Cougars to their hearts once more. They screamed for Bert Alschul to keep the rally alive. Jim, sitting between Charlie Overman and Art DeLeon, took off his cap and felt the hard lump on his head. "You think I was kidding?" he yelled at Strager. "Take a look!"

"On you it looks good," the manager said with a wry smile. "Yeah, Bruckner, I can almost see the imprint saying it was an official American League ball."

Jim clamped his teeth against his cud and turned his attention to the hitter. Alschul got in there when the relief man was ready, then topped the first pitch to the box. Jeremiah Jones, however, ran the count full, then belted the payoff pitch down the alley between left and center for a triple, bringing the crowd's racket to full pitch again. It broke off with a long-drawn-out soughing sound when Kershaw, ordered to squeeze, popped the ball into the air high enough for Toucette to race in and glove it.

Lenny Dee took over the pitching chores for the Cougars. The first man to face him was Dino Vita, and the Pilgrim cleanup hitter took one too high, another one below his knees. He looked at a curve that cost him, then pulled back just in time from an inside pitch. Vita stepped out and looked up at the Boston traffic man outside third. Then he stepped back in, took his wide stance and cut hard at Dee's fast ball. It came at Jim like a bullet, skipped through his legs and went out into right for a single. The fans booed the error, and the Pilgrim bench flayed Jim without mercy.

Trying to increase the slim, one-run lead, the Boston pilot put the bunt sign on for his catcher, Wilmot. The ball was bunted a little too hard just inside the first base line, and Jim charged in like a wild bull, scooped the ball up, and crashed head-on into Wilmot as he made the tag. He bounced back and hit the ground on his angel-bones, his lungs emptying painfully. Nausea made him retch as he tried to get to his feet. The Cougars flocked around him, the trainer's face registering first. When he was lifted up and walked around, he saw that Wilmot was still down, with the Pilgrim trainer working on his left leg.

Ossie Jameson picked up Jim with his blazing eyes. "You're a menace in a ball park, Bruckner!" he yelled. "If I had my way, you'd be thrown out of baseball."

Jim swung his glance toward Lenny Dee. "Give a dog a bad name," he griped, "and——"

Wilmot had to leave the game. Jim got a round of applause sprinkled with boos when he returned to first, dead certain that ninety per cent of the crowd figured he had deliberately roughed Wilmot up. Let them think so. Let them have their money's worth.

Lenny Dee disposed of the next two Boston batters, and Jim deliberately made his way in close enough to the Pilgrim bench to let them get their angry verbal shots into him at close range. He let them have it back, to the delight of the roaring crowd.

5 ⊜

A RUN BEHIND, ZACH JONES SHORTENED UP AND BUNTED THE ball between the mound and the third base line, and the Pilgrim pitcher made a good play but missed the runner by a step. The Boston infield still expected the bunt when Lenny Dee came up to the plate. Dee fouled the first pitch off, then let a chin-high pitch go by. He ducked under a low-bridge, the ball accidentally hitting his bat and bouncing out toward the mound. Zach Jones made second on the freak fielder's choice, and the racket in the stadium swelled when Jim took his place in the batter's box.

This was the clutch that separated the old pros from the greenhorns. This was where a man was supposed to hit. Jim felt he had to produce here, that the fans expected more than theatricals from him. He'd made the plays in the field, but he was no Fancy Dan. The Boston relief pitcher, Panken, missed with his first pitch, then blew one past the hitter. Jim swung hard at a knee-high pitch, then winced at the hostile note creeping into the crowd's noise. He stepped out, got dirt on his hands, clamped the hard hat tighter over his soft cap, and got set once more.

Panken fired. Jim watched the half-speed pitch come in and start to break. He cut at it and drove it into left center for a hit, driving Zach Jones in with the tieing run. Taking the wide turn around first, he indulged in a wide grin. That hit, he mused, was quite an insurance policy.

The Pilgrims, fired up, knocked Panken out. Jaciuk singled to right, sending Jim all the way to third, and Hank Bruda unloaded a triple to right center scoring Jim and putting the Cougars out in front, 7-5. Another fireman came in for Boston. His first pitch to Bert Alschul was skied deep to center, backing the Pilgrim fielder almost against the wall, and Hank practically walked in with the eighth Detroit run. Jeremiah Jones singled, but Kershaw forced him at second for the third out.

The ever-fickle fans gave the Cougars a big round of applause as they took the field in the top of the eighth. Playing wide of the bag, Jim mentally figured his batting average. Two for four today should bring him up close to .290. Only two other Cougars topped that mark. He felt five years younger as he yelled in at Lenny Dee to cut the Pilgrims down.

Stremski, leading off for the visitors, dragged a bunt on the third pitch, catching the Cougar defense flat-footed. Zach Jones tore in and finally picked up the roller, but saw he had no play. A pinch hitter, a forty-year-old veteran named Carrageen, came up to hit for the Boston pitcher. He let a pitch go by, then sent a high pop between first base and the stands. Jim gave it the full try, and came up short against the railing of a first base box just as it dropped out of reach. He caught a glimpse of a girl in a green dress, and heard her say, "He *is* chewing tobacco. What a filthy habit!"

Jim stared at the cigarette she held between her fingers. "Lady," he said, "you use the filthy weed your way and I'll use it mine." His eyes dropped, and he grinned. "And pull down your skirts. You're a big girl now." He trotted back to his position, leaving a burst of laughter in the vicinity of the first base box.

Stremski, the base runner, said, "Beauty and the beast. You get her phone number?"

60

"In your hat," Jim said, holding the man on. He glanced toward the seats, saw the girl in the green dress get up and make her way to an exit. If the people couldn't take it, he told himself, they shouldn't dish it out.

Carrageen sent a long, high drive to right center, but Jeremiah Jones caught up with it and made a sparkling, one-handed stab of the ball. Stremski, his team three runs behind, tagged up and raced for second, but Jones's slingshot arm cut him down. The two-ply killing put all the good strength in Dee's arm, and he struck out Kittredge, Boston's leadoff man.

The fourth Pilgrim pitcher retired Zach Jones, Lenny Dee, and Tex Loun in order. Strager, with the power of the Boston batting order due up in the first of the ninth, sent Lorber to first and a young outfielder named Monterosa to left field for defensive purposes. Jim followed Stan Jaciuk to the dressing room. Jaciuk said, "Thank the Lord that kid is only hitting .241. I could easily get the axe."

"You own left field and you know it," Jim said.

They weren't finished dressing before the Cougars flocked in. Jim got Overman's attention. "There was a big burst of noise out there. Somebody hit one?"

"Vita," Charlie said, "nobody on. We got it, 8-6."

The writers came in. One asked Jim if there was any truth in the rumor that the Detroit pro football club wanted him as a defensive lineman. "You're very funny," he replied, "almost as funny as your face, Tracy. How much blackmail do you make on the side with that scandal sheet?"

The writer's response was drowned out by Strager's deep baritone voice. The manager yelled at Hank Bruda and Lenny Dee, "Get goin'! You're late for the post-game TV show. Dermer is sweating it out."

"You're not on, Bruck?" Nabors, the columnist, shot at the first baseman-outfielder. "They must be nuts."

"That broadcaster is a college man," Jim said sourly. "He's afraid I might mispronounce some words or bite my nails or something. I might ask him how much pull he had to get such a soft job with the ball club."

"You just might be right," Bert Alschul said with a laugh.

Ed Stangaard took Overman by the arm and drew him aside. Jim, putting on his loud plaid sports coat, heard the pitcher say, "What are your plans for tonight, Charlie?"

"I figured on going to the wrestling matches with Jim, Ed. What's up?"

"My kid sister's in town, and she's wild about baseball. She's never met any major leaguers. I'm getting up a party of six or eight for the Harmony Club."

"Some other time, Ed," Overman said, and Jim called out, "Don't be silly, Charlie. Go right ahead. You can't get culture at a rasslin' match." He abruptly left the dressing room, kicking aside a small nylon bag that lay in his path. DeLeon yelled, "Hey, you——"

Outside the park, the young baseball buffs swarmed around him, and he impatiently waved them off. "I'm in a hurry. See me tomorrow," he snapped. They followed him to the street, where he hailed a cab, and some of them turned sour on him as the taxi rolled away.

He was in the apartment for almost half an hour before Overman arrived. Charlie eyed him warily, then turned a small smile loose. "Let's not make the last couple of days bad ones, Jim. Strager told me before I left that I was getting my unconditional release."

"Who's griping, Charlie?" Jim smiled back at the veteran. "The end of the road for you, and you're as happy as a bonus kid. How many men have felt that way? What'll I have when they dump me for keeps? Maybe a piece of a pool hall back on Halstead Street."

"I doubt that, Jim." Overman glanced at his watch, and quickly peeled off his shirt. "I have to step on it if I want to make that wingding at the Harmony Club."

62

"Have fun," Jim said. He turned on the TV to get the six forty-five news. The sports summary gave him the boost he needed at the moment. "Bruckner," the newscaster said, "knocked in the run that tied up the game and sparked the Cougars to a rally that sewed up the ball game. The stormy petrel, a great favorite of Detroit fans, set off a rhubarb in the sixth when Toucette, the Pilgrim first baseman, put a hard tag on him. Only prompt action on the part of the Detroit first base coach . . ."

He turned it off when Overman came out of the bathroom. "How did the Titans make out today?" Charlie asked.

"Don't spoil my night completely," Jim said. "Don't remind me of them."

After Overman had dropped him off downtown, Jim got himself a steak, then made his way to the Detroit Arena. A few minutes after he had taken his place in the line that strung toward the ticket window his eyes picked out a familiar figure among the crowd milling in the lobby. Jeremiah Jones stood a head taller than most people. Jim called out, "Hey, Jer'!"

The Cougar outfielder finally sifted Jim's voice out of the steady hum of talk, looked his way and flashed his big white teeth. He hurried over, and Jim said, "Give me some dough, Jer', and I'll get the tickets. Where's Zach?"

"That boy? He went to a church supper," Jeremiah said. "Anytime he smells that southern fried chicken, Jim, even if it's ten miles away, there is no holdin' him. How much for the ticket?"

Inside the arena they were shown to two seats ringside, eleven rows back and on the aisle. In the ring, a preliminary had already gotten under way. Jeremiah Jones had no sooner settled in his seat when trouble came from his immediate left. A half bald, thickset man with a pudgy, oily face slammed a paper beer container to the concrete and got to his feet. He turned his squinty eyes toward Jim. "You," he said belligerently, "change seats. I ain't sittin' next to him! You brought him, mister, so you——"

Jeremiah Jones started to get up. "It's okay, Jim. Let's not start anythin'."

"Stay where you are. You paid for that seat and nobody's going to push you around." He gently shoved Jeremiah back into his seat and leveled a meaningful glance at the contentious man. "I'm not looking for trouble, Buster, but if you want it . . ."

The big majority of the fans in the immediate vicinity backed up Jim's play, and made it plain to the beefy man that he should get lost and take his big mouth and unhealthy beliefs out into the street. Their heckling, along with the brew he had been drinking, triggered the man's temper and suddenly he climbed over Jeremiah Jones and made for Jim. Jim let him move in. He ducked a wild swing, then sent his fist deep into the man's paunch, bringing a painful gasp out of his adversary's throat. He followed up with a right hand to the breathless one's jaw, and caught the man as he fell across Jeremiah's lap. The police took over just as he got the man into the aisle and dumped him there.

The law, until it learned the true facts, was determined to remove the principals to the nearest jail. Jim quickly identified the dusky outfielder and himself, and a fan nearby shouted, "It *is* Jim Bruckner. That's Jones with him." The cash customers near ringside forgot the tugging and hauling of the two behemoths in the ring and rose from their seats to crane their necks for a glimpse of the big leaguers. Word of their presence spread throughout the big sports palace while the police forcibly removed the objectionable spectator.

Jeremiah turned a scared look toward his teammate. "This isn't so good, Jim. Man, that workin' press at ringside sure are lickin' their chops. They'll spread it on thick, and when Strager hears about it he'll hit the roof."

64

"Relax, Jer'. This kind of publicity you can't buy. We paid almost five bucks to see this show and I don't leave until I see how the Mad Moslem makes out against Rocky Gibraltar. I'll take Rocky if you care to risk a buck."

The Negro outfielder mopped at his face with a handkerchief. "I still wish I'd gone to that fried chicken supper."

When they left the arena an hour before midnight, and were fighting traffic in Jeremiah's second-hand Cadillac, the outfielder said, "I listened to your harpin' over what a tough time you had comin' up more'n once, Jim." He laughed briefly, and shook his head from side to side. "Brother, you just should've been with me and Zach. What happened back in that arena was just nothin', and you'd better believe it." He braked the car as a red light loomed up. "Don't get mad at me now, but I just got t' believe what a lot of the other Cougars say. Most of your tough times was made up inside your head. You'd rather kick a door down then turn a knob an' walk right through."

"The light's green," Jim said stiffly. "Get this heap moving."

"You should listen to your friends," Jeremiah said. "What you say to yourself all the time isn't doin' you any good. You don't get any useful arguments to the contrary."

"Sometimes you talk like the college guys," Jim ground out.

"I got two years in at Howard University," the ballplayer said. "An' baseball will get me that diploma. God bless the game. Amen."

Walking the two blocks from where Jeremiah had let him off, Jim was only vaguely aware of a tiny rift in his armor, and angry with himself for allowing Jeremiah's words to get under his skin just a little. I fought your battle tonight, my friend, he told himself. I fight for the whole ball club on the diamond. Name one man who ever fought for me. He was in the frame of mind that pleased him when he got into bed that night.

Jim was one of the first of the Cougars to reach the clubhouse the following afternoon. He was stripping off his coat

65

when Wally Bream came up. "Before you undress, Jim, Strager wants to see you."

Three lockers away, Jeremiah Jones shut his eyes and said, "Oh, oh! Mike's read the papers."

"Quite a story," Alschul said, grinning, as he came into the dressing room. "For once I'll admit you had a reason, Bruck. I wish I'd been there to get in a punch myself."

Bream said solemnly, "I don't think that's all Strager's got on his mind, Jim."

"Lots of luck," Jeremiah called out as Jim headed for the manager's office.

Mike Strager was busily shuffling some papers on his desk when Jim walked in. Without looking up he said, "Sit down, Bruckner." While the ballplayer cooled his heels, the Detroit pilot got a cigar going. He took a few puffs, then shoved his big chair back. "I hate to hit you with this, Jim," he said. "You're optioned out to Des Moines."

It took Jim a few moments to believe what he had heard. He felt the shock of the announcement in the pit of his stomach first. It traveled up to his throat and he had difficulty getting words out. It was anger and resentment that finally loosened his tongue. "I don't get it, Strager! I've been doing all right. If what happened last night——"

"It had nothing to do with this," Strager said. "In fact, everybody commends you for what you did. I can't honestly say I've loved you as a son or even a brother-in-law, but I did fight against this deal with the front office. I thought I had it licked up to yesterday's game, Bruckner, but you really cut your own throat."

"The Pilgrims played it rough with me, Mike! I had to protect myself. I didn't knock that Boston catcher over deliberately."

"You're still off base." Strager got up and paced the floor.

66

"Remember the foul popoff first, and the girl in the field box? You told her off and got a big laugh, remember?"

"She asked for it, Mike. But what has she got to do with——"

"Oh, you asked for it, too. Out of all the hundreds of dames in that ball park, you had to insult and embarrass Kay Lambert, the favorite niece of Sam Grayson, the owner of this ball club!"

Jim's mouth snapped open. Inwardly he railed against this underhanded trick of coincidence. Always, it seemed, the cards were stacked against him. How many times had he nearly filled a winning hand only to be slipped a deuce that was not wild?

"I'm sorry, Jim," Strager said. "Even though this club is on a build-with-youth kick, I thought I could hold you here. Udane, Overman, and Pedro Camacho are the other lop-offs. They figure Jaciuk can take care of left, and they want to see more of Lorber. After all, he cost them plenty. You're not finished by a long shot, Jim. We could recall you at any time. You're still Detroit property."

Jim leaned forward and banged a fist against the top of the desk. "Don't hand me that malarkey, Mike! They'll kick me around out there in the minors until they lose me. I'll tell you this: The fans won't like it. I've got a lot of them on my side and they'll yell to high heaven."

Strager nodded, a kind of compassion showing in his weathered eyes. "At first, Jim, but not for long. They forget easy. Take some advice, will you? Life is not like baseball. When you're finished with baseball you won't find umpires out there to tell you how or how not to play it. You won't get applause for bumping a guy off a sidewalk." He drew on his cigar, found it had gone out, and threw it out an open window. "Jim, a great catcher and a great guy who now rides a wheelchair said once, 'You have to be a man to be a big leaguer, but you have to have a lot of little boy in you, too.' I think your trouble is that you stopped being a boy after you were nine years old."

Jim swallowed hard when he became aware of the muted sound of the crowd filling the stadium. Faint bursts of talk and laughter drifting in from the dressing room were more painful than spike wounds. He had to call upon every last ounce of restraint lest he break loose and hurl Strager's desk upside down, and bury the manager under it. He could not remember when he'd cried last. He wanted to, now.

Strager's voice seemed to come out of a tunnel. "They want you in Des Moines no later than Tuesday, Jim. Only one thing more. That book you've got. Do yourself a favor and throw it away. It's ancient baseball history."

6 ☺

THE COUGARS, MOST OF THEM IN UNIFORM, WERE JUST SO
many faces to Jim Bruckner when he returned to clean out
his locker. In a voice that did not sound a bit like his own, he
announced, "I've got good news for you all. My head just
rolled."

A sudden quiet fell over the dressing room. Hank Bruda
soon broke it. "I wouldn't have bet on it, Jim." Jeremiah
Jones dropped a spiked shoe to the floor. "Not because of last
night?"

Jim, forcing a smile to stay on his face, shook his head.
"No," he said as a quartette of writers burst in. Singling out
Nabors, he asked the columnist if Mike Strager or Bob Vick
had given them the real reason for his being shipped out. "It's
a beaut," he said bitterly. "Make them tell you. If they don't,
give me a ring before Tuesday noon."

Jeremiah Jones cautioned him. "Don't sound off too much,
Jim. Don't dig yourself a deeper hole."

Ken Lorber, Del Stackpole, Kershaw, and DeLeon moved
in to express their good wishes and offer polite condolences,
and he brushed them off. "Say what's really on your minds!
The rough-neck, the mug, the grandstander is off your backs,
and it couldn't happen to a nicer guy."

"You said it—we didn't," Lorber returned under his breath,

and withdrew. Seasoned players like Hank Bruda, Alschul, Jaciuk, and Wes Ardwell did appear at a loss to understand the Cougar front office move. Sure, Bruckner was a brat, but an essential one. Subconsciously, perhaps, they were on the defensive regarding the Detroit club's accent on youth, for they were all past their thirtieth year. "I suppose they know what they're doing," Bert Alschul growled as he examined the strap on his catcher's mask. "All I know is I'm going to start saving my dough."

"How about us other orphans of the storm?" Charlie Overman called out as he and Al Udane entered the big room. "No crying towels left over for us?"

"Si," Pedro Camacho laughed as he removed a stack of comic books from his locker. He wanted to know if any of the other old men could use half a bottle of vitamin pills, then flashed his big smile at Jim. "How about you not going to Des Moines, amigo? I know where an hombre like you can make moch *dinero*. You an' me weel go back to my country an' start *revolucion*."

Strager's appearance scattered the talk and the laughter. "All right, break it up, and get out there," he ordered. "There's a game this afternoon." He took Jim aside before he left for the dugout. "If I were you, I'd have a talk with Bob Vick before I left town. Remember, this isn't the end of the line, and Griff Holley, the Hawkeye manager, is a real right guy. He could get through to you." He held out his hand. "No hard feelings?"

Jim's handshake was lukewarm. "Don't you see I'm almost dying laughing inside, Mike? Tell Vick for me I hope this ball club finishes in the cellar."

"Before you leave, you pigheaded brat," Strager roared, "tell Burkhardt to put your head under the diathermy machine." He snatched up his windbreaker and walked away.

Charlie Overman shook his head at Jim. "You will have to

70

hit four hundred with Des Moines to get back to this club."

"Who wants it? I can take care of myself, Charlie."

Udane snapped a bag shut. "Your only friend is yourself and you sure don't need an enemy, Bruck."

"How far down did they kick you, Al?"

"Pierre, South Dakota, Jim. Class A. I've been promised the manager's job there next year."

A little taken aback, Jim said scornfully. "That Kay Lambert must admire the way you comb your hair, Al."

Overman said, "Let's get a move on, Jim. A guy is coming to look at the apartment at four o'clock."

"You don't need me. I'm going out there and find a vacant seat and watch a couple of innings."

"Sure," Udane said, "I have a hunch I know why. Shall I paint your number on the back of your coat, Jim?"

Half an hour later, sitting behind the Cougar dugout, Jim received the deep satisfaction he'd been waiting for. Ken Lorber, with Alschul on second, and two out, went down swinging. The chant came out of the stands, "We wa-a-a-ant Br-r-r-r-ruckner!" Out in left field, a big cloth sign hung from the railing of the upper stands. It read: BRUCKNER, SI, VICK, NO!

Jim got up, took his time getting to a runway. A shrill voice cut through the crowd's steady racket. "Hey, there he is! There's Jim Bruckner!" The chain reaction followed. Hands reached toward him. The fans in the area let him know how they felt about his going. Bob Vick was a Pontius Pilate, a knucklehead. They told him to hit over three hundred at Des Moines and make a bum out of Mike Strager—that he'd be back before September.

Once back in the clubhouse, he finished cleaning his locker and stuffed a pack of scrap tobacco into his bag along with two gloves and a pair of scuffed spiked shoes. He tore an old photograph of Roaring Terry Flynn, spark plug of the old

71

St. Louis Alley Gang, off the inside wall, dropped it into his coat pocket and then took a last look around. With a big lump beginning to swell in his throat, he lost little time getting out of there.

When he reached the apartment Charlie Overman was busy emptying dresser drawers, whistling while he worked. The veteran's happy frame of mind aggravated Jim. "I heard you a block away, Charlie," he snapped. "Put on another record." He stripped to his shorts, snatched up part of the Sunday newspaper and threw himself on his bed.

Overman said, "That elastic bandage on your knee, Jim. If you don't need it, why wear it? Or is it another badge of courage, the sword scar from Heidelberg? Did it ever occur to you that you might be all wrong about the reason you're being sent down?"

"Not for a minute, Charlie."

Overman sighed with impatience. "I'm a statistic nut, Jim. You have only played in twenty ball games this season. The fewer times a guy goes to bat the higher his hitting percentage is. Your two-eighty-seven or thereabouts can't be compared to the same average of a guy who is in there swinging every day. You have knocked in nine runs, Jim, and booted four of them back to the other clubs. You've hung on because the fans go for your antics on the field. What happened to your long ball? Maybe Strager and the top brass figure your knee is a question mark and you really can't get that leverage at the plate."

Jim threw the newspaper aside. "Who asked for your opinion? As far as I'm concerned it isn't worth as much as a two-bit baseball. I'm still going to give the writers what I promised them. And will Grayson's face be red!"

"Nuts. You're thinking of your own publicity," Overman said. "It screens out your shortcomings. You've always preferred to get there by overaggressiveness, rather than by developing competence. Get wise to yourself, Jim."

72

"Save your head-shrinking for the kids at the baseball camp, Charlie!"

Overman continued with his packing, and Jim got up and turned on the TV. When the snow cleared, the screen revealed that Vita was at the plate for the Pilgrims. Stackpole was not on the mound for Detroit. "Vita," the voice of the Cougars, said, "has one hit so far in the game, a triple that scored three runs. It was the blow that finished Stackpole . . . Dee misses a breaking pitch and the count goes to three and one. The Pilgrims lead in this ball game, seven to two. . . . The base runners lead off—here's Dee's next pitch. . . . Vita cuts hard—it's a long drive to deep left center. Jaciuk runs toward the wall, but he'll never get that one. It's a home run for Vita, and the score now is ten to two in favor of Boston. That's all for Dee. . . ."

Overman bristled at Jim's pleased grin. "I don't know how I stuck it out here with you," he said.

After the Pilgrims' rally had been halted, when Jeremiah Jones opened Detroit's half of the frame with a single, the crowd booed Ken Lorber as he stepped in to hit. "Lorber has struck out and rolled to the box his first two trips, "Dermer announced, and his voice was drowned out by an insistent chant from the fans. "We wa-a-a-an't Bruckner!"

Overman angrily snapped a suitcase shut. A few moments later a great volume of sound spilled out into the room, and he turned to see the grin vanish from Jim's face. Dermer shouted excitedly, trying to make himself heard. "That one was sure tagged, far up into the stands in right. Lorber scores behind Jones, and what a grin he has on his face. Maybe that will start him off and——"

The crowd's racket thinned out. Somewhere, not too far from Dermer's mike, a fan yelled shrilly, "Who wants Bruckner?"

Overman discreetly remained silent, certain that he need

not remind Jim Bruckner of the fickleness of baseball fans everywhere. With them it was quickly off with the old and on with the new; out of sight, out of mind. Absence was not something that made their hearts grow fonder. They would swap a dozen old-fashioned singles and a rhubarb for the long bomb.

"It was about time," Jim muttered under his breath. "That Joe College was nothing for seventeen before he connected." He turned the set off. "Maybe we could have some kind of celebration this last night, Charlie."

"Sorry, Jim. I'm taking a train out at seven forty. At my age I'm not taking a chance that Vogel might change his mind overnight."

An hour later Overman was gone. Alone, Jim felt a few moments of panic. He was a man who needed an audience, be it one person or thirty thousand. Alone, a man had too much time for thinking. Things Overman had said returned to plague him when he went out to a restaurant. It occurred to him that he had not been getting as much good wood on the ball as of yore. Pitches he used to murder for distance had dropped in for singles or easy outs for opposing fielders. He'd had but two home runs with Detroit, one of them pure Ming dynasty.

A pretty blonde girl appeared and sat down at a piano. Her first selection was really long-hair, and a few of the customers, after a round of applause, requested something more lively.

Sure, Jim thought, his mood quickly changing, he'd give the customers at Des Moines what they wanted, too. The old rock and roll. Who expects typed actors to step out of character? Could Skelton play Hamlet? He grinned to himself. Sure, he was still valuable property to the Cougars. Otherwise they would have left no strings on him and most likely would have sent him down to Class A.

Leaving the restaurant where he'd fed a hungry confidence as well as an empty stomach, he decided to stick to the Bruckner pattern—please the crowd first. Griff Holley would have to go along with the click of the turnstiles.

Nabors called him late the next forenoon, and he did not hesitate to give the columnist the full details of his clash with the owner's niece. "Sure you can quote me," he said. "I've got what to lose? Listen, if I ever get back to the majors, don't bet it will be with the Cougars, even if I hit over four hundred with Des Moines. I'm a ba-a-a-d boy."

Jim snatched up a couple of early evening editions of the Detroit newspapers before he boarded the plane that afternoon. A tabloid had really reached for circulation by taking a recent photograph of Grayson's niece from its morgue and printing it on the first page. The headline read, *Bruckner out. Assist, Kay Lambert?* In true tabloid style, the incident had been gaudily colored. Words Jim had not used had been put in his mouth, and for once he almost regretted putting himself on record. Recognition by an airline stewardess, however, whisked away what qualms he might have had.

"Well," the smiling brunette said, "I see we both have been given a change of scenery, Jim. They took me off the Los Angeles flight over a month ago. That's quite a story in the *Star-Record*. Is it really true about Kay Lambert, or just something cooked up by the Detroit club's publicity department?"

"Most of it is true, Anne. Imagine me linked up with society. She will be burning right now."

The girl laughed. "Don't bet on it. It's the first time she's made the front page since she split up with that Hindu prince. By the way, how's that ape, Hank Bruda?"

"Still hoping, Anne. He still has your picture in his locker."

En route he studied the minor league standings. The Hawk-eyes were fifth in a six-club league, eight full games behind the Denver Steers. He'd played against them while with Omaha a year ago, and a few names came to his mind. Poke Hanna, Hal

Rettig, Bill Koch, and Faye Charlesworth. Griff Holley, he vaguely remembered, had come to Des Moines during the latter part of last season. He lay back and closed his eyes, a small grin playing around his mouth. This business was something like a chess game. One day you were a shining knight, and the next a pawn. Anytime you could expect to be rooked, especially if you got tangled up with a queen.

He took his own sweet time about calling the office of the Des Moines club. He waited until late the next morning before he picked up the phone, and after the usual welcoming clichés was instructed to call the Hawkeye manager at his home in the suburbs. He put the call through, and during the few moments of waiting that followed, let his eyes wander about the hotel room. Tomorrow, he said to himself, you will be living lower on the hog. Once in a while you might get a steak. Mostly when you're on the road, and . . . Holley's voice sat him up straight. "This is Jim Bruckner," he replied.

"Glad you're here, Jim. I'm going to be at the ball park at two o'clock. This club needs extra batting practice, and that's an understatement," Holley said. "I'd like you to be there—give us a chance to talk and let you meet the players." He laughed. "No, I don't expect you to swing at any."

"I'll be there," Jim said.

When he came out of the elevator, Des Moines writers intercepted him, firing questions. He parried them all, making it plain that he was making no statements, one way or the other, for at least a week. "You've read your own newspapers," he told them, "Well, nothing happened to me since I left Detroit—only a little airsickness. Sure, I'll most likely play tonight."

He saw no reason for hurrying. After lunch he sat around the lobby until nearly two o'clock, basking in a luxury he would soon have to forego to a certain degree. The Hawkeyes' dressing room was empty when he arrived at the ball park, save for a Man Friday, one of whose many duties was to watch over the players' personal belongings. His hair was thinning out and he had a cauliflower ear. "You must be Jim Bruckner," he said in a gravelly voice. "Glad to meet you."

"Yeah. But don't be too sure." Jim drank in the smell of a freshly-mopped floor, of the medication and countless rubbing preparations and healthy sweat that the showers had not fully washed away. Big league or bush, the smell was always the same.

He made his way to the home dugout, the chatter of voices and the sound of wood crashing against horsehide coming to meet him. Several of the Hawkeyes were hovering around the batting cage; four were out on the field, and the rest were in the dugout's shade. A tall, rangy man, watching the hitters closely, suddenly turned his face toward him. The sun flashed on the glasses he wore and turned the gray at his temples to patches of bright silver. Griff Holley's sun-baked face was gaunt, with the prominent cheekbones of an Indian.

"Your name must be Griff Holley," Jim said, and the Hawk-eye players got up from the bench.

Holley came off the step and held out his hand. "Sometimes I wish it wasn't," he said with a dry smile. "Glad to have you here, Bruckner." He turned toward the other Hawkeyes and ran off half a dozen names—Lingersen, Kern, Arida, Schaefer, Hanna, and Shea.

Two of them Jim remembered. They had not forgotten him. Poke Hanna nodded. "Don't bother, Griff. I got scars to remember him by. Just let me say I'm glad he's on our side."

"Remember when I tipped your bat in Omaha?" Hal Rettig, a catcher asked, smiling at the recollection. "You piled into me. We both got thrown out. Tell me, Bruck. Did you really try to get that Lambert dame's phone number?"

"Let's drop that," Jim said flatly, and sat down on the bench to watch a tall and lean Hawkeye take his cuts in the batting cage. Holley said, "Rettig, you and Kern get out there and swing your bats. Neither of you have been breaking any fences." He dropped down next to Jim and remained silent for fully a minute. "Your knee, Jim," he finally asked, "is it all right? Or did Vick pull a fast one on me? They took a pretty fair outfielder away from me to make room for you."

"Let's say the Cougars are mostly scholars and gentlemen, Mr. Holley, and I'm not either one. Maybe they figured that was reason enough."

"Well, you're here. I hope you can help us," Holley said, then quickly got to his feet and trotted out to the batting cage, where Rettig was limping around after hitting himself on the foot with a batted ball.

"Bow-wow-wow!" chorused the other Hawkeyes.

7 ☺

WATCHING THE HAWKEYE WORKOUT ABSTRACTEDLY, JIM
was uncertain of his first analysis of the Des Moines manager.
Eyeglasses on a man had never failed to stir a negative reaction
inside him, but there was something about Griff Holley that
shunted this old aversion aside. When he'd shaken hands,
Holley's grin had not been lopsided, and the man's eyes had
not held that "or else" expression. For once he was reluctant
to admit that Strager might have been right.

Holley came back into the shade of the dugout, shaking his
head. "Did you see that knucklehead, Kern, trying to stand
like The Man out there, Jim? What won't a guy do to get out
of a slump?" He wiped his face and neck with a towel and said,
"Let's go to my office."

It was a small, cluttered-up place, the walls covered with
photographs, one of them a real eyecatcher. It was a group
photograph that quickened Jim's pulse, a facsimile of the one
in the front of the book written by Roaring Terry Flynn. He
glanced toward Holley, then back at the picture, and a grin
flickered across his face. The Des Moines manager, he told
himself, was a kindred spirit. Jim Bruckner was "in like
Flynn."

"That was a great team," Jim said as he sat down in an old
leather chair. "Maybe the greatest."

"I doubt that," Holley said. "A war was on, and most of the top stars were either flying a plane or carrying a gun. They were maybe the strongest team in a weak league, and I would not bet they'd finish seventh today in a ten club league."

Jim's eyes heated up. "If that's what you think of them, why the picture, Griff?"

Holley laughed. "A reminder that I once made the big leagues. I was with that club for six weeks but was long gone before they won their first pennant. Let's say I wasn't tough enough to stick with them."

"You knew Terry Flynn? Mitch Drummond, and Cass Trumbull?"

Holley nodded, his eyes studying Jim closely. "I read Flynn's book, Jim, and I'll still take Goldilocks and her three bears. Like all autobiographies, especially by sports hot shots, Flynn's was colored up by a ghost writer who played cat and mouse with the truth. Take that business where Mitch Drummond challenged a fan to meet him out in the parking area after a game in Pittsburgh. What the book said about Mitch prevailing was all wrong. The fan almost took Mitch apart."

Jim stiffened in his chair, and his eyes stormed up. "It's sure funny to me, Holley, that no other big leaguer seemed to know about that. They certainly would have told me."

"Would you disillusion a kid if he asked you if King Arthur and his knights really got licked more times than they won? That once in a while they robbed the people of the country-side, or——"

"Like you said—you couldn't hold your own with the Alley Gang, Holley. So you've been knocking them ever since."

Griff Holley smiled, and showed not the slightest bit of resentment. "Maybe I asked for that, Jim. But let's get down to tonight's game with the Little Rock Travelers. If I didn't start you in left tonight I'd be torn apart. The stories in the late afternoon papers will drive a couple more thousand people

80

out to the ball park." He got up and smiled down at the new Hawkeye fielder. "Don't try too hard, Jim."

When he returned to the hotel, Jim picked up a Des Moines newspaper and retired to a remote corner of the lobby to go over the sports page. A writer had devoted his column to Jim Bruckner's past exploits on the diamond. "Bruckner's former teammates, from what this writer has gathered, never exactly applauded his high-jinks or undue aggressiveness on or off the playing field. Although the fans and the majority of the working press have always taken him to their hearts because he is colorful, they often consider him an incorrigible—something of an overgrown juvenile delinquent. They click their tongues at some of his shenanigans, yet revel in his deviltry.

"How will Bruckner react to being sent down to the minors again? Will it take off a little, maybe too much, of his aggressiveness and turn him into an everyday, matter-of-fact performer? Local fans will not hesitate to tell you that they have too many of these in the Hawkeye club. They'll lose no time convincing Griff Holley that they want the real Jim Bruckner, not a converted model."

Don't try too hard. Holley's advice had not exactly been an admonition. Once, a long way back, a man had said Jim had promise, but that it would never be fulfilled if he kept hamming it up. All at once Jim felt he was caught off base, involved in a mental rundown. Which way would he run? He forced himself to think back to his worse days, to draw his chains around him and pull them tight. He had to agree with the sports writer; he had to be the real Jim Bruckner, and give the fans the fireworks they expected. There was very little doubt in his mind that certain minor leaguers would not be the least bit timid about applying the match.

The rest of the day passed only too quickly, and a knot was drawing tight in his stomach when, shortly after seven o'clock, he entered the Hawkeye dressing room. Hal Rettig and Poke

Hanna, along with half a dozen other Des Moines players, were undressing in front of the row of lockers. Both Rettig and Hanna greeted him with a passingly friendly smile and a "Hello, Jim." The others simply nodded, regarding him both curiously and dubiously. Once again he felt like a trespasser as he let his utility bag thump to the floor. The clubhouse attendant came out of Holley's office. "There's a locker with your name on it, Jim," he said. "Your monkey suit's hangin' up there. You got Arida's old number. Seven."

"Okay, thanks." So who was Arida? He located his locker, stored a few personal belongings on the top shelf, then placed his spiked shoes and fielder's glove on the long wooden bench. Poke Hanna, the Hawkeye shortstop, said, "The crowd's starting to come in already. With you here, Bruck, the management won't have to give no TV sets or dishes away tonight."

Jim turned a small grin Hanna's way and then as quickly erased it from his face. The nervous sweat formed cold patches under his arms and knees, and he reached for his scrap tobacco. The taste of it steadied him. The lump it formed on the side of his face, he knew, struck awe in some of the youngsters here. More college boys! Some of them seemed just about graduated from bubble gum.

Hal Rettig chuckled. "There's a breeze blowin' out there tonight, Jim. Better check its direction before you get up at bat. You could make that ump blinder than he really is if you just happened to let go with some——"

A ripple of laughter broke some of the ice. Conversation built up and banter ran back and forth. The dressing room seemed to have shrunk when the entire roster of the Des Moines club was checked in. Jim was wondering how small that park out there would look after his visits to the big city baseball plants when Griff Holley came in. The manager checked as to whether or not Jim Bruckner had been introduced all around, then said, "We're getting a big crowd tonight.

Over nine thousand. So let's show some hustle. Let's make Jim feel at home."

An uncomfortable silence followed. The inference, although Jim felt sure it was not intentional, was there, and his neck burned red. Griff Holley quickly cleared the atmosphere. "Let's begin to play some real baseball, and start climbing."

"A rough night to begin, Griff," Nick Umbric, a player-coach, said with a wry smile. "They're pitchin' Halka tonight."

Soon it was time for the Hawkeyes to move out. When they filled their dugout, the Travelers were taking spirited infield practice, and Jim swept the minor league layout with his eyes, never remembering a bigger Central League crowd or a noisier one. When the fans recognized Griff Holley they yelled at him, asking him if Bruckner was going to play. "Trot him out, Griff," a feminine voice shrilled, "Let's see the big bad man!"

"Yeah, where's Bruckner?"

The Hawkeye bench jockeys ribbed the Little Rocks when the visitors took over in the batting cage, Poke Hanna needling the loudest. One of the enemy, a hefty man with a big nose and bowed legs, took a few steps toward the dugout and shouted, "You feel pretty cocky tonight, huh, Poke? Because you got that poor man's Ty Cobb with you?"

Jim's blood heated up. It was time, he thought, to make his presence known to one and all. It was expected of him. He moved out in front of the dugout and shouted at the top of his voice, "With those legs, big mouth, how do you get your pants on?"

Behind the home dugout the fans roared with pure delight. "And with that nose, you don't need a bottle opener," Jim added.

The bowlegged man glared at him. Suddenly the Little Rock player grinned, displaying a big space between his two front teeth. "Yeah, Bruckner," he said, "you're just like they say you are. I hope you got plenty of insurance." He turned and strolled back to the batting cage, the fans still buzzing.

"That was Benny Knauf," Chet Kern offered when Jim sat down. "Nobody in this league tangles with him unless it's at a ping-pong table, Bruckner."

"I'll try and remember." Jim gave Griff Holley a quick glance but read no sign of disapproval on the manager's tanned face. A few minutes later he was shagging the fungoes Holley was hitting to left field, aware that he was no picture of grace. The fans applauded every catch he made, particularly the one where he ended up in a sitting position. Faye Charlesworth, the center fielder, helped him up. "I should've warned you about that spot. It's an old drainage ditch they didn't cover over with enough dirt, Bruck."

"Some pasture," Jim snapped. "When do they let the cows in?"

When the Hawkeyes came in from the field, Jim took a close look at the tall lefty warming up for the Travelers. He was young, as pliant as a buggy-whip. Hal Rettig, putting on his shin-guards, also had his eyes on Halka. "He's got eleven wins and one loss. Three times he's taken us, twice by shut-outs."

"Then why haven't the New York Titans bought him?" Jim asked a little sourly. He looked up at the clock above the scoreboard in right field, and it told him he would be out there playing for the marbles in less than two minutes. The public address system suddenly came to life, the announcer's amplified voice cutting through the crowd's steady racket. Very little re-action came from the fans during the run-down of the opposing lineups until the announcer came to the number three spot in the Des Moines batting order.

". . . In left field, wearing number seven, Jim Br-r-ruckner-r-r-r-r!"

The response was explosive. It lasted until Griff Holley

came back from the pre-game conference at the plate. Jim stared down at the floor of the dugout, hoping that his sudden attack of the jitters was not showing, and fully aware of the boos that went along with the cheers. An atmosphere he had tasted many times before pervaded the Hawkeye dugout, and he felt that intangible pressure of the thinking of the other players. Men like Rettig, Lingersen, Poke Hanna, and Kern had been favorites here for a long time. They could not be expected to regard the man who was stealing their thunder as a "white-haired" boy.

Griff Holley's sharp voice shook him to his feet. "All right, let's go!" Before he cleared the dugout he felt the slap of Holley's hand against his backside. "Good luck, Jim," the manager called after him.

His legs were trembling when he took over a much-trampled spot in left field. The fans were not too far away from him here and all their remarks, encouraging or otherwise, were very distinct. He concentrated on ignoring them, peered over at Charlesworth or in at Hal Rettig, for these old veterans had their books on opposing hitters. Pete Nicola got behind on the Travelers' leadoff man, caught up with him and then induced him to hit a fly ball to left. Jim raced in a few steps, then back-pedaled before he got a bead on the ball, and gathered it in. The crowd applauded.

A left-handed hitter faced Nicola, and Jim instinctively moved to his right. Faye Charlesworth waved him back. "De-Grossa hits a lot to the opposite field, Jim," he shouted.

DeGrossa popped up to Hal Retting on the second pitch, and Jim grinned as Benny Knauf moved out of the on-deck circle with a gait that reminded him of a duck's waddle. Nicola, before he pitched to the big first baseman, turned and checked the positions of the Hawkeye picketmen. Jim took the cue, moving deeper along with Charlesworth and Bill Koch.

Knauf made Nicola work. He ran the count full, then fouled

off four pitches. Holley's right-hander made the big man wait, then threw him a change-up. Knauf timed it right and drove it to deep center, where Charlesworth caught it with his back against the fence.

The fans urged Poke Hanna to get on when the leadoff man for Des Moines stepped in to hit. He had earned his nickname by the safe hits he'd poked through enemy infields. Jim, hitting in the all-important third spot in Holley's batting order, leaned against the bat rack and watched Halka closely. When the southpaw hummed two fast balls past Poke, he wiped his moist palms against the front of his shirt. He had never seen faster stuff anywhere.

Halka wasted a pitch and tried to get the batter to bite at a pitch just under his chin. With the count even, Hanna just stuck out his bat at a fast ball and poked it over the Little Rock shortstop's head for a single. Jim made his way to the on-deck circle, the fans yelling as much for him as the hit Poke had made. Their noise ebbed when Halka struck out Koch, then rose to high tide when Jim Bruckner dug a foothold in the batter's box. The Travelers' bench came abusively alive. Bronsky, the Little Rock receiver, was anything but an introvert himself. "Hello, Busher. You don't look so tough to me."

Jim aimed tobacco juice close to Bronsky's shoes, then immediately swung his head around and looked out at Halka. The fans were still roaring over the byplay when Halka blazed his first pitch in for a called strike. Jim stepped out, looked askance at the umpire, and shook his head. "Every move a picture, you bum!" Bronsky said.

Halka slowly rubbed up the ball. He peered down the pike at Bronsky, and nodded. The ball came in high and fast and sent Jim sprawling into the dirt. An angry note came into the crowd's roar as he slowly got to his feet. He glanced at the man in blue and saw not a trace of compassion. He grinned to himself. *Okay, you just play along with Bruckner.*

Halka went to work again. He fired over to first, once, twice, to hold Poke on. He came in with a sharp-breaking curve that Jim fouled back into the screen. Ahead of the hitter, the south-paw elected to take his time, to wage a cold war. He fooled with the rosin bag, removed his cap, and sleeved his brow. He adjusted the cuffs of his pants. When he was about to fire again, Jim stepped out. Again Halka made the hitter wait. Again Jim stepped out when Halka was about to work once more, and the umpire gave him a warning. "All right," he shouted back, "Make that bed-slat out there pitch!" Griff Holley came running to the plate to demand equal rights while nine-thousand-odd fans yelled themselves hoarse. This was what they'd paid to see.

Comparative quiet restored, Jim took his wide stance and waited for Halka's next pitch. It was a slider, too low. Bronsky growled at the umpire's call, and bent over to get dirt on his hands. Jim said, "You sound like a zoo at feeding time."

A curve came in. It started to hang, and Jim took a full cut, certain he would ride the ball far. It sliced off the end of his bat and dropped inside the right field foul-line just out of reach of the Little Rock fielders. Poke raced to third, and the Des Moines fans were on their feet and howling. With the long ball hitter, George Lingersen, at the plate, they anticipated an early shower for Halka.

Jim took his lead off first, finally drawing a throw. He hur-riedly jumped back to the bag, bumping Benny Knauf hard and causing him to drop the ball. Knauf jawed at him angrily, and Jim made a palms-outward gesture as if to ask everybody in the ball park, "What's with him?"

Lingersen got ahead of Halka, two balls and a strike, then smashed a scorcher to the right side of the infield that the Little Rock second baseman had to dig out on the edge of the outfield grass. Running hard, Jim hit the dirt just as the Trav-elers' shortstop took the throw to the keystone sack, and bowled the man over before he could double up Lingersen at first. Poke Hanna scored on the play.

The Little Rock infielder got up slowly and brushed himself off. "Until we meet again, Bruckner," he said coldly just before Jim trotted off the diamond. A great round of applause showered him as he ducked into the dugout. The reception from the Hawkeyes was something else again. He was not sure if he had impressed them or shaken them up with his style of play.

They favored him with uncertain smiles as he sat down next to Poke. Griff Holley said, after Hal Rettig fouled a pitch into the crowd back of third, "How have you lived so long, Jim?"

He was thinking of an appropriate answer when the crack of Rettig's bat brought him to his feet with the others. The Little Rock right fielder, Cluney, was running at top speed toward the fence. He suddenly skidded to a stop and waved his gloved hand at the ball that fell into the seats. The big catcher, after scoring behind Lingersen, received a roaring welcome in the dugout. Bedlam had broken loose in the stands. Jim, after shaking Rettig's hand, settled back on the bench soberly. That long bomb had already made the fans forget what he had done thus far. He could never afford to let up for a moment, and for the first time in his life, he knew he was running a little scared.

Well, he had triggered this early rally. He yelled at Halka with the others, and the Little Rock pitcher walked Dutch Schaefer. Faye Charlesworth slammed a hit through the middle, and the Travelers' pilot hurried out to the mound and signaled for a right-hander. "The first time since last year that we've belted him out," Hal Rettig said. "Maybe our luck *has* changed."

The Hawkeyes had a five run bulge when they took the field. A fan shouted at Jim as he trotted past third, "Looks like you got the lead out of 'em, Bruckner."

8 ⊖

PETE NICOLA WAS STILL WORKING ON A SHUTOUT WHEN THE
Hawkeyes came in for their turns at bat in the last of the fifth,
and he drew a nice round of applause when he walked to the
plate to lead off. Since the first-inning fireworks, very little
had happened to excite the crowd. Already conceding the first
out—Nicola had made only two hits since the start of the season—they sat back to give their lungs a rest. A few moments
later, a clean single to left by Nicola had them stirring again.
The rhythmic clapping of hands and stamping of feet greeted
Poke Hanna as he stepped in.

The Little Rock pitcher, Amara, his infield alerted for the
bunt, kept his pitches high. A curve wide of the plate put him
far behind, three and nothing. Poke stepped out, checked with
Nick Umbric, coaching at third, moved back in, and struck
out on three pitched balls. Jim moved to the on-deck circle
just vacated by Bill Koch, drawing an expectant roar from the
fans. Resting on one knee, swinging a bat over his head, he
immediately became the target for half a dozen Travelers
bunched on the top step of their dugout.

Jim welcomed the stinging going-over they gave him. He
was onstage. He reached deep into his own salty vocabulary
and threw mild insults back at the bench jockeys. He sent a
thin clothesline of tobacco juice in the general direction of the

Little Rock dugout, and it was doubtful if half the people in the ball park were watching Koch take his cuts. Anything could happen here. Jim Bruckner, at any moment, might storm out of the waiting station and challenge the entire Little Rock bench.

As if the brain-waves of the spectators struck blips from a built-in radar inside his head, Jim suddenly moved out of the on-deck circle and took a few threatening steps toward the enemy hecklers. The umpire called time, took off his mask, and shouted a stern warning, and Jim jumped back into the on-deck circle like a frightened doe. The stands still spilled laughter when Koch laced a single into center. Bronsky, the Little Rock catcher, made himself heard above the crowd's lusty roar when Jim smoothed out the dirt in the batter's box. "Ha, it's Barrymore again. Lights—cameras! Your make-up is on crooked, Bruckner."

"You've got a big league mouth, Bronk," Jim snapped, "but a Class C brain." He dug in and looked out at Amara. A junkman, they called the Little Rock reliever. His stuff came at you as big as a beach ball, but when you swung, it turned into an aspirin tablet. The last time up he had cut a slow curve with all his might and had flied to shallow right.

With two strikes against him and only one ball, Jim crowded the plate. Amara turned loose an infrequent fast ball that nearly scraped his chin, and he staggered back from the plate. Bronsky laughed through his mask. Jim stepped out and jawed at Amara, drawing a barrage from the Little Rock bench. The fans reacted as he'd expected. He took his time getting back in, and the umpire warned him again, then gave Amara the signal to throw. Jim had little time for getting set before the letter-high pitch floated in. He swung, driving a sizzler to deep short. The Little Rock fielder knocked the ball down, scrambled to his feet and fired it across the diamond to Knauf.

Jim slid hard into the bag as Knauf lunged for the shortstop's low throw close to the foul line, and he kicked the ball out of the big man's glove. Knauf, as the umpire flashed the safe sign, let out an angry bellow and threw his first baseman's mitt at the base runner, and Jim, seeing that the ball had rolled a few feet away, took off for second base. Meanwhile, Nicola rounded third and scored, and Koch slid into third. Knauf, having recovered the ball, threw wild trying to nail Koch, and the Hawkeye right fielder raced in with the Hawkeyes' seventh run. Jim wound up at third. Over across the diamond, Harv Kelsoe, the Little Rock manager, and four other Travelers were half-dragging Benny Knauf toward his dugout. Kelsoe was throwing heated words over his shoulder at the umpire. The Little Rock third baseman kicked up some dirt close to the bag and snapped at Jim, "You're not a young rooster, Bruckner. How long do you think you can stand that pace?"

"As long as I have to, kid."

A new pitcher was brought in for Little Rock, and Lingersen greeted him with a long sacrifice fly that brought Jim in. Hod Elmo, a veteran reserve outfielder, said, "Bruckner, I believe all I've heard. You could toss a stone into a river and cause a flood. One thing I'm sure of and that's that I don't intend to walk down a street with you tonight."

"They gave that shortstop an error," Jim griped. "Anywhere else it would have been a hit. Maybe the owner's wife does the scoring."

Hal Rettig skied out, and the Hawkeyes took the field with an 8-0 lead. Pete Nicola retired three Little Rock hitters in order, and it was not until the first of the eighth, with the score unchanged, that he ran into trouble. With one out, he hit McNeil, the Little Rock shortstop, with a pitch. Poke Hanna bobbled an easy double play ball, and Bronsky came up. Jim moved back with the other outfielders, respecting the big catcher's power. Nicola worked carefully, feeding Bronsky breaking stuff. With the count even a two and two he turned a pitch loose he quickly wished he could have snatched back.

Bronsky got all the good wood against the high and outside pitch. The ball sailed to deep left center and Jim started running along with Charlesworth. The crowd screamed a warning when it seemed they would crash together close to the barrier. Above the racket, Jim heard Nick yell that he would take it, and he put on the brakes only a few running steps from the big center fielder. He saw Nick reach up for the ball. It bounced off his glove, and Jim lunged forward and caught it a foot from the ground. His momentum carried him almost to the fence, and from there he fired the relay in to Poke Hanna. The base runners, unaware that the ball had not dropped in, were on their way home. Poke's throw to second doubled up McNeil.

Jim Bruckner had to admit it was the luckiest catch he'd ever made as he ran in from the outfield amid thunderous applause. Pete Nicola was the first to reach for his hand. He thanked Jim for the great save. Griff Holley slapped the ex-Cougar on the shoulder, then said quietly, "That was Nick's ball all the way, Jim."

"I try for anything within reach, Griff," Jim fired at the manager. "I don't know any other way."

The favorite sons in the dugout were beginning to feel the damage to their pride. Bruckner, with only one dinky hit, had stolen the show. For the rest of the game they gave him the silent treatment. While he was out in left during the first of the ninth, they pulled him apart. "A grandstander for sure," Hod Elmo said, "a real brat on spikes. Griff, why did they palm him off on you?"

The manager gave Elmo an impatient glance. "He's a ball-player, Hod. It isn't so much the things he does as the way he does it. Do you deny he brought results tonight?"

"Ask me that a month from now, Griff."

92

Ray Scott, a rookie, said his piece. "He doesn't play baseball, Griff. He fights it like it was some kind of a war."

"Try and get along with him," the manager said as he watched Nicola get the final out of the ball game.

On the way to the dressing room with Nick Umbric, who had played five years in the majors, Griff Holley asked, "Well, what do you think of him?"

"Bruckner? The crowd loves him. What else matters, Griff? If he hits his usual average, doesn't drop too many flies, and stays alive, he might earn his keep."

"You don't like him, Nick."

"He's a feller you could like and hate both at the same time. One way or the other, Bruckner couldn't care less."

Jim had no sooner come out of the shower room when the writers crowded around him. They threw stock questions his way and he reminded them that their fraternal brothers on bigger newspapers had already supplied the answers themselves. "Like I read in one of your rags this morning," he said, "I didn't come here to get converted, but to play this game the way I've always played it. Like——"

"Roaring Terry Flynn and his alley gang," a graying veteran writer offered. They say that book he wrote is your bible, Bruckner."

"Yeah. It is a book that says to turn the other cheek when somebody belts you, but having run out of cheeks you are free to knock somebody's brains out." Jim got up from the bench, turned toward his locker, and then suddenly spun around. "I play baseball the way it used to be played, like a hungry ballplayer. I hate to lose, and if my own mother tried to put the tag on me sliding home I would knock her over. If you want nice, refined copy, talk to the Joe Colleges here."

Ray Scott and Lew Paskert, two bonus kids recently sent down to Class AAA for further development, seemed on the

93

verge of arguing the point violently when Hal Rettig and three other Hawkeyes moved in to calm them down.

"It wasn't anythin' personal," Jim said, throwing the rookies his maddening smile. "If somebody had offered me even five thousand bucks just to sign, and the contract called for my selling my soul to the devil, I wouldn't have hesitated. It's just that nobody can tell me that a young ballplayer already softened up with twenty-five or fifty grand is going to bother going all out." The dubious smile on the veteran scribe's face angered him. "All right, you look it up, mister. How many of them made it big? Not even one out of ten!"

"Okay, Bruckner. Maybe you're right, but it's the way they operate today and you can't fight it."

"And I don't have to like it," Jim said. "Now, let me get dressed."

The sports pages the next morning inferred that his presence on the Hawkeyes alone had had much to do with the eight to nothing shutout of Little Rock. He touched off the spark when it was needed; he made his own breaks. Perhaps his great catch had involved a certain amount of luck, but the fact remained that it happened. Bruckner, last night, had the fans on the edge of their seats—had them asking themselves, "What will he do next?"

Jim spent most of the day looking for an efficiency apartment, and it was very late in the day when he found one that lived up to the advertisement. He used up another hour moving in, and by the time he'd had a bite to eat it was seven thirty. The Hawkeyes had just finished batting practice when he arrived at the dugout. "So I'm late, Holley," he said, beating the manager to the punch, "I had to look for a place to live."

Griff Holley's displeasure turned to impatience. "You could have taken your time. No one asked you to check out of the hotel, did they?"

"I don't want to owe anybody anything," Jim said, and

moved toward the water cooler. Cooling his throat, he looked out at the Little Rock pitcher warming up. "Who is he?" he asked.

"Sid Trotman," Umbric said. "If he has his control he can be tough. Look, Jim, if he throws them in too close, believe me, he doesn't mean it. He's a nice guy."

"No guy is nice when you play against him." He went out in front of the dugout and got a look at the crowd. It was bigger and noisier than the night before and he was tempted to ask Holley when he'd get a share of the gate. The fans, the Little Rock jockeys, were giving him the attention he craved as he ducked back in out of sight. A few minutes later, when he took his place in left, he tipped his hat to the big round of applause.

The Travelers got to Holley's starter, Wally Scherr, in a hurry. A single, a walk, and an error by Lingersen filled the bases after one man was retired. Bronsky looked at a called strike, then drilled a pitch against the left field wall. Jim let the ricochet get away from him and Faye Charlesworth had to run it down, and before he could get the ball back to the infield, three runs crossed the plate. A fan shouted, "It's him. Old Iron Glove!" and the majority of the customers, willing to forgive and forget for the moment, lustily shouted him down.

Scherr took a long look toward left field, kicked up some dirt, then turned around and went to work. He bowed his neck and got two more outs, leaving Bronsky glued to third.

"Let's get 'em back," Holley said, clapping his hands as Poke Hanna walked to the plate.

Jim thought he should say something. "I haven't played billiards for a while, Griff. I'll get the hang of that wall."

The Hawkeye players just stared out at the Little Rock pitcher, Trotman, hoping he would start in wild. Their wishes, father to their thoughts, came true. Trotman walked Poke on five pitched balls and hit Koch on the arm. The fans came fully alive when Jim left the on-deck circle. Trotman looked toward the visitors' bullpen, where two reliefers were already tuning up, knowing the hook would most likely be his if he lost the third man up. He came in with a fast ball that Jim let go by for a called strike. His next pitch was low.

Trotman got a new ball, rubbed it up and got set to pitch again. He went into his motion, quickly whirled, and fired to first, getting Koch before he could slide back into the bag. The Little Rock base runner, his ears red, got the full treatment from the fans as he returned to the bench. Trotman went to work again, and fired one above Jim's chin that had smoke on it. A slider followed and Jim got only a small piece of it. With the count at two and two, he left the batter's box to get the pine tar rag in the on-deck circle.

Lingersen, waiting to hit, tossed it to him. "Get on, Bruck," he said. "I feel a big hit coming. I always murder this guy."

Jim took a long look at Trotman when he stepped in again. The pitcher had the face of a choir boy, and he was certain he could be conned. He crouched close to the plate, narrowing the strike zone, and the umpire warned him. He swung his head around. "Your job is to call the balls and strikes," he called out, "not to tell me how to earn my living."

A chuckle came out of Bronsky's mask. "Don't make me like you, Bruckner," he ground out. The fans were in an uproar.

Trotman hummed one in that sent Jim staggering back from the plate, and the ex-big leaguer walked halfway to the mound, and yelled, "Just one more, Buster, and I'll shove your glove down your throat."

"It wasn't intentional," the Little Rock hurler said. "I'm sorry."

Nice polite boy, Jim told himself. I've got him in my pocket.

The umpire warned him when he got back in. "One more demonstration, Bruckner, and you're out of the game."

Jim ignored the man. He crouched over the plate and gave

Trotman his toughest look. The pitcher threw wide of the plate and Jim trotted to first. Big George Lingersen followed up with a drive that went clear out of sight, and the game was all tied up. After the boisterous bench welcome for Lingersen, Jim, seated next to Hod Elmo, made himself heard above the crowd's noise. "That kid out there won't last long. He should have thrown right at my head."

"I sure would have," Hod said. Jim, sensing that the utility man's remark had met with solid approval the length of the dugout, let a small laugh escape him. "Then there is some of the old breed left in you guys. You should use more of it." He shifted his eyes toward Griff Holley to see if his remarks had gotten a rise out of the manager. Holley, intent on getting another run or two, shouting encouragement out at Hal Rettig, did not even look his way.

Trotman went all the way with the big Hawkeye catcher, then threw him a change of pace that struck him out. A few moments later, Dutch Schaefer lined deep to center, and the long first inning was over. The pitchers settled down, and neither side could threaten until the last of the seventh. Starting things off for the Hawkeyes, Poke Hanna punched a single through the middle, and the partisans urged Billy Koch to hit the leadoff man along. Koch worked the string out, then popped to the Little Rock shortstop. Again Jim drew a round of applause as he took his place in the batter's box. In three times at bat he had failed to hit, and more than a few of the fans let him know it.

Trotman fooled him with a change-up, then brushed him back with a pitch in tight. In came the curve ball, and he swung hard when it started to break over the outside corner. The ball clotheslined into right for a single, and Poke ran around to third.

Lingersen, the Des Moines cleanup man, worked Trotman to a full count, fouled off three "pay-off" pitches, then slammed a fast ball to deep short. A double killing seemed certain when the Traveler fielder dug it out, whirled, and fired to his second baseman. Anticipating the take-out slide on the part of Jim Bruckner, who had never let up on his running despite the sure force, the keystone man jumped two feet off the ground before firing to Knauf, the Little Rock third baseman. The ball hit the dirt and took a crazy bounce over Knauf's shoulder, and Poke Hanna scored the lead run.

Chet Kern, on the bench, wagged his head unbelievingly from side to side as he watched Lingersen take second. When Jim reached the dugout he grinned at Griff Holley. "I had a hunch he'd throw wild. How could he know I wouldn't slide in?"

"You sure know how to skin a cat many ways, Jim," the manager said. "You are a real con man."

Hal Rettig drove the Little Rock left fielder far back to haul in his long drive, and the Hawkeyes ran out to the field to protect a one run lead. The error on the part of the Little Rock second baseman proved to be the difference, Trotman refusing to let an enemy get on for the last two frames. In the dressing room later, a writer pointed out that, during the course of the game, Jim had turned what had seemed to be two certain outs into two runs.

"Lingersen helped him a little with his bat," Dutch Schaefer called out. "Sorry, just thought I'd mention it, Harry."

Jim, bent over lacing a shoe, winced at the quality of the laughter running the length of the room. This was the story of his baseball life—a favorite with the fans, just something to be tolerated in a locker room. He was beginning to feel the wear and tear deep down inside him.

9 ⊜

THE DES MOINES CLUB WON FOUR OF THEIR NEXT SIX GAMES
and moved into fourth place, two games and a half behind the
Topeka Chiefs. Although Jim's batting average was down to
.264, the sports writers gave him the lion's share of the credit
for the Hawkeyes' reversal of form, and the increased attendance at the ball park. He had put the much-needed bonfire
under Griff Hollcy's team, had stung their pride and forced
them to play to the last ounce of their ability. They resented
the press he had been getting and wanted some for themselves.

"Bruckner is not wearing out the league's pitching by any
stretch of the imagination," Harry Frankel, *Des Moines Star-
Record* columnist, wrote, "but he has a dozen other ways to
beat the opposition besides with a bat. His fielding has been
described as weird; he has the faculty (or is it showmanship?)
to make the usually routine catch look sensational. Since he's
admittedly a disciple of the old St. Louis Alley Gang, it is
every opposing infielder for himself when he runs the bases.
Every umpire, to his way of thinking, wears a black mask and
carries a gun.

"The Hawkeyes will board the club's twin-engined Convair
tomorrow and fly to Memphis, the first stop on an eleven game
road trip. . . ."

It was a hot and humid July night. It was also Sunday and there was very little for a loner to do on such a night but go to a movie. Jim, bored with the newspapers and his own company, suddenly felt the need of Charlie Overman's calm but critical voice, and Jeremiah Jones's loud and hearty laugh. That the other Hawkeye players were in no great hurry to include him in their off-the-diamond activities was as plain as his dwindling batting average. He sat down by an open window and looked out over the city, and let himself dwell upon the early days of struggle, most of which seemed to have stretched into extra innings. Inwardly he had to remain an angry man. Turn soft and they would certainly knock him back to where he had started. That afternoon he hadn't exactly stolen the show. The Topeka pitchers had held him to one hit in four official trips to the plate, and he had lost a fly ball in the sun that gave the Chiefs two runs. He'd had to compensate by accusing the Chiefs' catcher of tipping his bat, and a real rhubarb had followed. He'd drawn his biggest burst of applause of the afternoon when the umpire threw him out.

He leaned back in his chair, his eyes half closed, trying to discount his worries. One day, he mused, a guy would make a lot of money with a book telling ballplayers how to get out of a slump. He remembered some hitters who never did recover their batting eyes, and felt a momentary panic. During the last few days, some fat pitches had been served up to him, just begging to be driven against or over the barriers, and he had either fouled them off or popped them up within easy reach of the opposing fielders. What was it Mike Strager had said in so many words? "You'll have to put your bat where your mouth is."

His fielding had never been more than adequate, something he always figured could never get any worse, but during the last few arc-light games he'd had difficulty judging the flight of routine drives to the left field area. Two nights ago, a lofty fly ball had sailed into left center, with two out, and two enemy base runners on the move. He'd gone after it, but Charlesworth had come racing over from center, yelling, "Get away, Bruck. I'll take it."

Jim left the apartment house and took a walk to a small park several blocks away. He corrected that statement by Mike Strager in his mind. He would have to put his bat where his glove wasn't. He had only partially grasped some of the things the writers had said about him. What did they mean he was a reactionary who linked himself with the past rather than the future? That he was like a spoiled kid who, if he yelled loud enough, held his breath until he got red in the face and kicked up his heels, would get the attention he needed? Who told those writers they were head shrinkers?

There were times when Jim Bruckner condescended to count a blessing or two. He was only one step down from the top of the ladder, and the Des Moines club was owned by one of the richest men this side of Texas. J. K. Blakely was a real baseball buff and went to extreme lengths to make his ballplayers happy despite their position in the Central League standing. He flew them on the long hauls in his Convair, and the short-haul bus was air-conditioned and fitted out with indoor plumbing. Salaries and hotel accommodations on the road were not too far removed from major league standards.

His thoughts turned to a narrower channel. How far from Class AA was a .260 hitter? Even from Class A? A man went downhill much faster than he could climb up. He knew he had to consider the possibility of the fans' wanting competence on his part along with rock and sock aggressiveness. The public even tires of a top comedian's jokes and antics, given too big a dose. And if the Hawkeyes began losing once more, the writers would say Bruckner's fire had burned out.

101

Walking slowly back to his apartment, Jim built up his resentment against the present scheme of things. He would have to keep battling his way. This world was a jungle.

The flight to Memphis was bumpy, and Jim hoped it wasn't a bad omen. The Hawkeyes, prodded by Harry Frankel, making the trip with the club, talked mostly of the trade they were in and the respective talents of their contemporaries. "It's really a sound profession today. When I was a kid they used to look upon professional ballplayers as so many characters too lazy to go to work."

Jim straightened in his seat, swung his head around and made his voice heard above the roar of the engines. "That's what this game lacks today, Frankel. Characters, so-called. Who have you got today to stack up against Terry Flynn or Bobo Humphry? How many of these Joe Colleges or sound business men give the fans a laugh? A lot of players look like they are wound up like a toy before they're sent out of the dugout."

"You should complain, Bruckner," Frankel replied. "You've got no competition."

Laughs came from the plane's midsection. Dutch Schaefer, sitting with Jim, put a restraining hand on the outfielder's arm. "Hold it down, Bruck. He can hurt you," he warned.

"How did those two characters turn out, Bruckner?" Frankel asked mockingly. "Flynn became a night watchman in a warehouse in Chicago, and if I'm not greatly mistaken, Bobo lives today mostly on relief checks."

Jim, more disillusioned than angry, clamped his teeth together and stared straight ahead.

Later that day, when the Hawkeyes piled aboard the bus that was to take them to the hotel in Memphis, Frankel made it a point to drop into a seat next to Jim. "I'm sorry, Bruckner, if I was a little too free with the needle on the plane."

102

"Forget it," Jim said, and forced a smile.

"I read Flynn's book. There was some real funny stuff in it. Especially that business of Bobo with the apple. He peeled it in the dressing room, took it out with him to the mound, and threw it for his first pitch. The batter swung and spattered it over the catcher and the umpire. They were going to throw Bobo out and he said to the umpire, 'Show me in the rule book where it says a pitcher can't throw the old apple.'"

Jim chuckled. "Yeah, but that one about six of them building a bonfire in front of the dugout in St. Louis with the thermometer reading ninety-eight in the shade, and warming their hands over it—it must have been a riot."

"Well, time has to change, Jim," Frankel said, "even if not for the best. We can't lick 'em; we have to join 'em. Good luck tomorrow night."

Jim found himself sharing a room with Nick Umbric, and he had the feeling right away that Griff Holley had not picked a roomie for him at random. Umbric represented fatherly advice; he was a steadying influence. The veteran had a wife and three kids back in Des Moines. An hour before dinner, Griff Holley came into the room, peered through his glasses at Jim, and nodded pleasantly. "Nick, I think we should change some of our signals," he said to Umbric. "Stop by my room in the morning and we'll go over them." He turned his glance toward Jim again. "I overheard you and Frankel on the bus. About Bobo and that apple——"

"What about it, Griff?"

"Oh, that guy liked apples, but he never threw one to a batter. He did peel one in the dressing room to eat before he went out. Then he cut his finger and couldn't throw a ball for almost a week. One thing I admit: Bobo also liked fermented apple juice too much."

"What's the angle?" Jim asked Umbric when Holley left. "Why is he trying to downgrade those guys—Flynn and——"

"Good reading is often more important than facts, Jim. You ever read about Paul Bunyan?"

"Who did he play for?"

Umbric grinned. "He was a much bigger man with an axe than a big league general manager. Look, you believe what you want, kid. Like I've always said, everybody should have their heroes. You'd better go and shave."

"I shaved this morning," Jim snapped.

"All right," Umbric replied angrily, "Look like a bum. Act like a bum!" He snatched up a clean shirt from the back of a chair and hurried into the bathroom. Before he shut the door behind him he threw a parting shot at his roommate. "You're a good actor, Bruck, but Bobo was better."

The Memphis stadium was nearly filled five minutes before game time the following night. The Grays were in first place, and Jim Bruckner was with the visitors. Half a dozen photographers distracted the Hawkeyes when they took batting practice, and Jim, when they singled him out, was glad he hadn't shaved, and that he had put a little more tobacco in his cheek than usual. Memphis badgering experts got on him as he posed. "Hey, Bruckner, show 'em your muscles. The ones in your head! No wonder you scared that Lambert cupcake!"

Getting back under cover, Jim anticipated a rugged night. This was a hostile crowd that had made no bones about letting him know it. They would applaud the lumps he received and would boo his accomplishments. "That Abendroth looks awful fast tonight," Poke Hanna said. "I've had only one hit off him all year."

"Swing at his first pitch," Griff Holley said, moving along the front of the bench.

Abendroth, the Grays' bellwether, leading all Central League pitchers with a gaudy 1.89 earned-run average, finished warming up. Holley's pitching choice, Cal Kimbroch, kept firing. There wasn't a vacant seat in the park when the National Anthem was played, and the people in downtown Memphis must have heard the full roar of the fans when Poke Hanna walked up to the plate to start things off for the Hawkeyes.

Abendroth reared back and threw a fast ball over the heart of the plate and Poke took his cut and lined it to the Grays' right fielder. Billy Koch stepped in, also swung at the Southpaw's first pitch and fouled it into the seats. The Memphis catcher trotted out with a new ball and held a brief conference with his battery mate. Jim stared at him intently as he came walking back, and suddenly remembered something he had read during yesterday's flight from Des Moines. "Hey, Nethercott, I read where they're going to make you pay your wife alimony," he called out from the on-deck circle.

The Grays receiver broke his stride, glared at Jim, then moved to his position behind the plate. The umpire looked Jim's way for a long moment, then gave Abendroth the go-ahead. The Grays' bench, the partisan crowd, reacted more violently to his needling of Nethercott than Jim had expected. He grinned into the dirt.

Abendroth hummed a second strike past Billy Koch, then failed to cross him with a pitch wide of the plate. Jim yelled at the Memphis catcher, "How many starving kids have you got, Gus?"

Nethercott was steaming. He banged his mitt into the dirt before the next pitch came in. It was a bullet, and Billy Koch swung and missed. The ball got by Nethercott, and the Hawkeyes' speedy right fielder raced to first base. Nethercott seemed on the verge of clashing with Jim as the Number Three hitter in Holley's lineup approached the plate. "Keep your big mouth shut, Bruckner," he raged, "or I'll have Billy fill it with a baseball!"

105

The fans were up and howling. Boos, catcalls, the entire range of a crowd's abuse, showered down on Jim as he waggled his bat at Abendroth. The southpaw peered in for his catcher's sign, nodded and grinned. The fast one burned in close, rocking the hitter back on his heels. The next pitch sailed under Jim's chin, and Nethercott said through his mask, "The next three you won't even see, Showboat."

"Look, see how scared I am, Gus," Jim threw back, and crouched low over the plate. Abendroth's slider was called a ball, and he came down from the hill, jawing a protest. Jim stepped out, picked up some dirt and grinned over at Lingersen, waiting to hit. Back in, he crowded the plate again, giving the Grays' southpaw a margin for error. Abendroth got a piece of the inside corner of the plate with his fast ball, and also of the batter's sleeve. Trotting to first base, Jim looked back over his shoulder, and laughed at Nethercott's beef with the umpire.

Lingersen, following orders, cut at the first pitch and slammed it to left center for a single. When the Grays' picketman bobbled the ball on the first hop, Jim tore for third. The play would be close, he knew, and as he hit the dirt he threw his body in the path of the ball. It bounced off his shoulder and rolled toward the stands, and he got up and raced home. Reaching the dugout, he heard Ray Scott, the rookie infielder, remark above the fan's racket, "He can do more by doing nothing than any man I ever saw."

"Don't tell me, Bruck," Hod Elmo said while Hal Rettig got behind the Memphis southpaw, two strikes and a ball, "that you engineered that one. It was pure luck and——"

"I get them any way I can," Jim said, and then jumped to his feet when Hal Rettig, getting the fever, lashed a hit through a hole in the left side of the Grays' infield. Lingersen scored, and the Memphis manager hurried to the mound.

106

"Two hits off the guy in one inning," Poke Hanna said, shaking his head. He threw Jim a look of begrudging admiration. "Bruckner, you could shake up the Kremlin."

Abendroth stayed in and began working on Dutch Schaefer, and Holley's bench jockeys worked on him in turn. Schaefer worked the count to a ball and strike, then fouled the third pitch off. Abendroth missed with a curve, then gave the Hawkeye second baseman a big motion and yanked back on the string. Dutch watched the ball float in, and let it alone. The umpire called it a ball, and the Grays' southpaw threw his glove halfway to the plate and stormed in from the mound. The man in blue whipped off his mask and ordered him back. Abendroth kept coming, shouting his opinion of umpires who needed glasses but refused to wear them. Before Nethercott, the Memphis pilot, and three of the Grays could move in to contain him, Abendroth was given the sign that he could go and get his shower.

An ugly note crept into the timbre of the crowd's noise as Abendroth slowly walked off. Paper cups flew out of the seats. A seat cushion spun toward the umpire, and the Memphis catcher blocked it with his mitt. Park police became fully alert when some of the fans threatened to spill out over the diamond, but when a warning funneled through the P. A. system that the game would be forfeited to the visitors if order was not restored, peace finally prevailed.

His warm-up pitches over, the Memphis fireman, Jack Clausson, fired the pay-off pitch to Schaefer and caught him looking. Running out to the picket line alongside Charlesworth, Jim shouted, "If a ball comes out there I think belongs to me, Faye, stay away. I won't give up on it."

"I get the message," the center fielder replied. "Neither will I."

Cal Kimbroch forced the first two Grays to ground out. The

Hawkeye outfield moved back and shaded to the left when the Memphis left fielder, Janovski, dug a foothold in the batter's box. Kimbroch slipped a strike past the slugger, then came in with a pitch the big Pole liked. He drove it high and deep to left, and Jim back-pedaled to the warning track, his eyes gauging the flight of the ball. For a moment he lost it, then found it again, and had to run in on the outfield grass, for it was not carrying as far as he thought it would. Suddenly it was off to his left and he had to compensate in a hurry, finally gloving the ball with a last desperate effort, a foot off the ground.

Faye Charlesworth, having put on the brakes a few feet away, started laughing. "If that was an act, Bruckner, you're a cinch for the Sullivan show," he said as he ran in. The fans jeered Jim as he followed Faye in. A few thousand were laughing. A man in a box behind third shouted at the top of his lungs, "Now show us the Indian rope trick, you humpty-dumpty!"

"Who can lend me a heart pill?" Kimbroch asked, giving Jim a sour look as the outfielder entered the dugout.

Six innings later, the big Hawkeye right-hander was still pitching his heart out, grimly hanging on to a shutout. He had two men out and a runner on first in the last of the seventh when the Grays' best pinch hitter sent a looping drive to left. Jim came racing in, tried a shoestring catch, and missed, but Charlesworth coming over fast, cut the ball off, and fired a bullet to Poke Hanna. Poke rifled it into Rettig, and the Memphis base runner, trying to score, was nailed a foot from the plate.

After the Hawkeyes had failed to pick up an insurance run in the top of the eighth, Jim reached for his glove. "That's all for the night, Jim," Griff Holley said, and gave Lew Paskert the nod. The defensive move shook the ex-Cougar up. It hardened the bulge in his right cheek and shot a pang of misgiving through his meridian. He hadn't hit a ball out of the infield and he'd looked forward to his fourth time at bat. His inner turmoil worsened when his replacement hit a single in the first of the ninth. There was little jubilation in him when Cal Kimbroch finally walked off the mound with a sparkling 2-0 shutout of the league leaders.

10 ⚾

THE HAWKEYES WERE WASHED AND GETTING INTO THEIR
street clothes when Hod Elmo answered a loud knock on the
door of the dressing room. Jim clearly heard an alien voice
above the other noises. "Gus Nethercott sent me to tell Bruckner he'd meet him out in the parking area in ten minutes. On
the west side. That is, if Bruckner has the guts."

Nick Umbric hurried to the small cubicle the Memphis club
reserved for visiting managers just as Jim yelled, "Tell that
bozo I'll be there." Hal Rettig and Faye Charlesworth has-
tened to assure Jim they would go along with him, and he
shook his head. "I never needed help from anybody. I don't
need it now!"

Griff Holley came out of the office. "Bruckner, I want to
talk to you," he shouted. "Come in here!"

For the next two minutes, the manager of the Hawkeyes
gave Jim no chance to utter a word. "You think I'm going to
let you break your hands on Nethercott's hard skull, Bruckner?
Oh, I don't blame the guy. It's one thing to needle a man about
the way he walks or because of a big nose, but when you make
aspersions about his personal life, that's something else again.
There is a big difference between a joke and an insult, and I'm
advising you to put a soft pedal on that sharp tongue of yours.
You tangle with Nethercott and I'll fine you a hundred dollars
and hit you with a five-day suspension."

"Didn't you hear some of the things they called me tonight, Griff?" Jim retorted, raising his own voice.

"Don't you ask for it, Jim? Wouldn't you resent it if they singled out some other guy on this club for a target?" Holley took off his thick-lensed glasses and laid them on the desk, wearily rubbed his eyes. Jim stared at the glasses, and hardly knowing why, was seized with an almost uncontrollable impulse to shatter them with a fist.

"All right," he said through a dry grin, "so I like to be noticed, Griff. Has it hurt the gate any?"

Holley replaced his eyeglasses and stared at Jim for fully thirty seconds. "It's hurting you, Jim. Deep down inside, you hate a lot of the things you do. You're in a state of constant rebellion, and pretty soon it will be too late for you to bring out the legitimate baseball talent that I know is in you. That's all, Jim. I meant what I said. Leave Nethercott alone."

After breakfast the next morning, Jim picked up a morning paper and discovered that writers could throw from the port side, too, and shave a man close. One sports expert's stint was loaded with lefthanded compliments. "Abendroth," he wrote, "has a temperament made to order for the likes of Jim Bruckner. He got himself out early and the Hawkeyes went on to win. Bruckner's very presence in a ball park seems to stir up contention. Even the fans appear susceptible to his rowdyism, and watching him perform last night, a lot of them must have ceased to wonder why the Detroit Cougars cut him loose. With Bruckner in the lineup, Griff Holley has to go along with two and a half outfielders . . ."

The Memphis catcher hit back through a late afternoon paper. As he'd expected, Bruckner had backed down. He was all mouth. He was a real busher under a thick skin.

"There should be quite a mob out tonight," Nick Umbric said. "The fans smell blood—your blood, Jim."

"I should have called Holley's bluff," Jim griped. "I never ran away from a fight before."

"I'll buy that, Jim. You always run after one." He sat down on his bed and studied his roomie for a moment. "Look, I've known Griff for a long time. He doesn't talk too much, but when he does he means it! And don't ever call *his* bluff. He'll never deal you another hand."

When Poke Hanna walked to the plate to lead off for Des Moines that night, they were selling standing room at the ticket booth. Thousands of early arrivals were already hoarse from their heckling of the Hawkeye outfielder every time they spotted him outside the visitors' dugout. Extra police were in evidence.

Long Tom Silva, who had affectionately been dubbed "Dry Bones" by other players in the league, induced Poke to ground out, short to first, and Jim picked a bat out of the rack and strolled to the on-deck circle, the doubtful din of welcome making his ears both burn and ring. He knelt down, caught the shine of Nethercott's eyes through the catcher's mask, and then swung his glance toward the Grays' pitcher.

Billy Koch struck out, and as he walked away the crowd turned loose a stinging, jeering blast he knew was not meant for him. Digging in against Silva, Jim kept his eyes away from Nethercott—kept his lips shut tight. He grinned to himself. He would give the alien crowd the unexpected; he would play it down.

He let a good pitch go by and rammed Silva's second delivery just outside first. From behind the screen, a voice bellowed, "You sure scared the brat, Gus! H-e-e-ey, Bruckner, you're yellow!"

Jim guessed right on the next two pitches. Silva's half-speed curve swept in, ripe for killing, and he took a full cut. The ball sliced in safely to the opposite field, and the crowd's noise tapered off a little. "You're smarter'n I thought," Frazer, the Grays' first baseman, said as he moved in to hold the runner on. "Gus would have torn you apart."

Jim ignored the remark and kept his eyes on Lingersen at the plate. Silva got a strike over on the Hawkeye cleanup hitter and then threw a soft one that Lingersen skied to shallow center. The Grays' second baseman ran out; their center fielder sprinted in. There was a collision, and the ball fell in untouched. Jim, with two out, running with the pitch, ignored Nick Umbric's traffic signal at third and tore for the plate. The Memphis center fielder's throw came in on a line to Nethercott, and the big backstop hurled himself at Jim, blocked him off the plate and rammed the ball violently against his ribs.

Jim rolled in the dirt, his lungs drained of air. A pain shot through his chest and he felt nausea. Dimly he heard the approving roar of the fans as Hawkeye players grouped around him. From a far distance he heard Griff Holley's angry voice. "Gus, that was a cheap shot!" He tried to struggle to his feet, but felt the restraining pressure of many hands. They stretched him out, and the fog lifted. He felt burning anger along with the pain in his rib cage.

Tim Shea, Hawkeye trainer as well as coach, said, "Easy, Jim. Stay put. If the rib is busted——"

When he finally got to his feet and turned his eyes toward Nethercott, he was amazed to see that there was concern plainly written on the blocky face. Big Gus suddenly turned away and walked to his dugout, angrily firing his mask ahead of him. Helping Jim off the field, Griff Holley said, "The boos you hear, Jim—for once they're not all for you."

Before going to the dressing room he paused in the dugout to take a few deep breaths. The pain, he was sure, was letting up. He swept his eyes along the row of faces of the players who had not taken the field and was not surprised when they

114

clearly told him he had asked for what he'd received. "I know," he said. "A rookie told me once, 'He who lives by the sword,' and all that."

The voice over the P. A. system was requesting the services of any physician who might be in the stands as he made the rest of the way to the dressing room with Tim Shea. The cold sweat came out on him when Shea said, "It could have been your leg, or an arm, Jim. You were lucky." He helped the outfielder out of his uniform shirt, and onto the table. "Don't ever believe all you read. Gus got a bad deal from his wife and the courts. He's a real nice guy if you meet him halfway."

"I did, Nick. I'm lucky to be alive."

Nearly fifteen minutes later a doctor came in with Hod Elmo and introduced himself. Five minutes later he assured Jim that he had suffered nothing worse than a couple of bruised ribs. "Use cold compresses at first," he told Shea. "Then any good rubbing solution that contains plenty of alcohol. No arnica, even though the skin isn't broken."

The doctor had no sooner left when Pete Nicola, his uniform dark with sweat, came into the dressing room and threw his glove against the wall. "Four-nothing," he said angrily. "They murdered me. I left two on and only one out for Tom Ellstrom." He hurriedly stripped and headed for the shower. "If I don't come out inside half an hour, forget it. Just phone my family."

Elmo tarried for a few moments. "The only hit we've had so far was a single by Lew Paskert," he said. Jim winced, but not from the pressure of Shea's fingers. He had to admit that the rookie was as graceful as a gazelle out in the field, and he thanked his lucky stars that the twenty-year-old kid had much to learn swinging a bat. Staring up at the ceiling, he knew he could not afford to stay out of uniform too long.

"You sure carry a lot of battle scars, Jim," Shea said, drying his hands with a towel.

115

"Inside and out, Tim." He sat up and forced back a grunt of pain. "I shouldn't be out long?"

"You'll know better in the morning." Tim Shea hid his grin from the outfielder. "The fans here are going to miss you, in a way." The noise of the crowd suddenly swelled, and he shook his head. "The Grays must be getting to Tom."

Ellstrom came in five minutes later. He had been around too long to let an occasional reversal gripe him. "The ball has eyes for those guys tonight," he said with a wry smile, and went to the Coke machine.

Pete Nicola came out of the shower room and regarded the veteran fireman askance. "Well, what happened?"

"The two men you put on, Pete? They were driven in," Ellstrom said, and gave Jim his attention. "You really did get ribbed tonight, huh, Bruck?"

"Yeah." Jim nodded and slid off the table. "It's the only laugh I've given you guys since I got here."

Ellstrom winked at Tim Shea. "Why, we love you, Jim. We just aren't the demonstrative type."

Jim ground his teeth together, crossed the room and turned on the radio again. ". . . and that inside the park home run makes the score nine to two in favor of the Grays. Holley's out of the dugout again to talk to Jose Acosta, the Hawkeyes' third pitcher. Bill Horan, a right-hander, is warming up in the visitors' bullpen. Looks like Acosta will stay in. Holley figures there's no use to lock the stable after the horse is stolen. . . ."

Jim snapped the transistor off and began to dress. Out there the crowd was still in full voice, acclaiming the long ball. The fans would be reminded of the first-inning incident only when they read the papers in the morning. At this moment, Jim Bruckner failed to exist in their collective minds. He felt a moment of panic.

The sky was leaden the next morning, promising to wash

out the third game of the series, and Jim hoped old Jupe Pluvius had more than a threat of rain in his mind when he got out of bed. The bruise, high on his left side, had turned bluish-black during the night. It was still painful. Nick Umbric, already up and dressed, grinned at him. "It'll turn greenish-blue next, Bruck. You would look good on color TV. Better shake a leg. We're supposed to get down to breakfast no later than nine o'clock."

Jim was struggling into his sports coat when the telephone rang. Umbric answered it, then held the instrument out to his roommate. "It's for you," he said.

"Who would call me? Is it Griff, Nick?" Jim spoke into the phone, "Yeah?"

"Bruckner, this is Gus Nethercott. I had no right to clobber you like I did last night. I've been run ragged, what with one thing or another, the last couple of weeks. I——"

Jim laughed. "Look, Gus, don't get soft or the word will get around," and as he threw Nick an amused glance, Nethercott's words got hot in his ear.

"All right, I've told you, Bruckner. Now go soak your big fat head!"

Jim cradled the phone, his face split by a smug grin. "That was Nethercott, Nick. Imagine it—the bum apologized to me. Wait until I see the writers."

Umbric's eyes gathered storm clouds. His neck reddened. "You make one crack to them and I will personally take you apart, you knothead. Frankly, I don't think Gus should be sorry for what he did to you. Let me tell you something else, Bruckner! You're a menace to polite society. You have the power of an adult and the responses and motives of an infant. After this road trip I'm going to tell Griff to inflict somebody else on you, or I'll quit the club."

Jim's face sobered and he felt his hard surface cracking in places under the impact of Umbric's words. A trickle of

117

repentance escaped, but as usual he came up with a reply he did not really mean. "Do that, Nick. I'll try to bear up under it."

The player-coach, however, saw a telltale expression in Jim's eyes. It reminded him of the same look he'd seen in the eyes of a cocker spaniel he'd once had to reprimand. He grinned and slapped the stormy petrel on the rear. "Forget what I said. Let's get our bacon and eggs."

Jim was in uniform that night, watching Hod Elmo play left field for the Hawkeyes. Paskert was .098 against left-handers. Wally Scherr was going along with a 1-0 lead in the last of the third when the rains came, sending the fans in the cheaper seats to cover. Both dugouts sweated out the delay for more than a half hour before the word came that the game was postponed until a future date. "It better clear up before tomorrow at eight," Chet Kern said, as the players reached the dressing room, "or I don't get in no airplane."

Hod Elmo turned toward Jim. "You know they have some-thing new in Denver. They've got an altitude of five thous-and feet there, and they've got tanks of oygen in both dugouts in case the players start passing out. For guys like Nick Umbric and Tom Ellstrom they have pulmotors."

Griff Holley sought Jim out and inquired about his sore ribs. "They feel okay, Griff," the outfielder said. "I could have gone right back into that game. Heck, Joe Kendig once played a whole game for St. Louis with a fractured leg."

"No kidding, Jim? As I remember it, he faked the injury to con the opposition. He stole two bases before they got wise to him. Against the Chicago Bruins, I think it was."

Jim abruptly walked away from the manager, kicking a catcher's shin-guard out of his path. Griff Holley watched him for a moment, a twinkle in his eyes. He'd have to apologize again to that group picture hanging back in his office in the Des Moines ball park after the road trip. There were times

118

when a man had to do certain things he did not like to do, like playing fast and loose with the truth about the old Alley Gang.

The Hawkeyes were airborne before nine the next morning, and when the seat belts were unfastened, Tim Shea passed out the dramomine pills. Jose Acosta's face, the color of the roasted coffee beans of his native Colombia, always turned a shade paler in flight. "Only one place I care to go sky-high ees on peetcher's mound," he said, eagerly gulping two of the pills. "Thees flyeeng ees only for the swallows from Capistrano, si."

The Convair bucked in the teeth of a brisk head wind, and Jim tried to get his mind off the turbulence with a newspaper. The situation in the Far East was threatening to boil over again, there were more threatened strikes, and there was an axe-murder in New York. He quickly turned to the sports page where the world was always in balance. Mike Strager's Cougars had dropped to eighth place in the American League, and the New York Titans were ahead of the pack by seven and a half games. A column captioned "Goode's Sports" drew his full attention, and he read a lengthy quote credited to Gus Nethercott:

". . . I'll admit I went off half-cocked when I tagged Bruckner out, and deserved censure from the writers and the fans. I called him on the phone the next day and offered an apology. I would not say Bruckner accepted it, but as far as I'm concerned the incident is closed."

Jim leaned his head back against the seat pillow and closed his eyes. One part of his mind told him he should have met Nethercott halfway, but another forcibly reminded him that he had never given any quarter to the opposition and had never asked for any. He had established that code long ago, and not until he had fully recovered his batting eye could he even consider letting up even a little with his unique methods of pleasing the crowd.

119

Across the aisle, three seats back, Hod Elmo was making book on the Denver Steers. They were just a game and a half behind Memphis, and as a club led the league in hitting. "We'll get DeCorsia tonight," Elmo predicted," and that new south-paw, Johnny Mundt, in either one of tomorrow's twi-night affairs. I won't mind sitting it out with DeCorsia in there. How many games we win against the Steers so far—two?"

"Don't worry, Hod," Paskert, the brash rookie, called out, "we didn't have a fire under us then."

Jim heard the thrust abstractedly. He was thinking of those fat pitches he had been missing with alarming regularity, of the tricks fly balls had played on him as they came his way in the outfield. Could a man only thirty lose his skills overnight? He felt a sudden sinking sensation in his stomach although the Convair was now flying smooth and easy.

11 ⊖

THAT NIGHT, JUST BEFORE THE HAWKEYES' BUS WAS TO LEAVE
for the Denver Stadium, Nick Umbric picked up a few pieces
of mail at the hotel desk. One letter made his rugged face
shine, and Jim felt a stab of envy. What little mail he'd ever
received either came from insurance companies or magazine
circulation managers. Nick said, "It's from my kid, Freddie."

Nick stuffed it into his pocket when he heard Griff Holley
call out, "Okay, let's get aboard. Get the show on the road."

Jim, nearly a half hour later, watched Nick's face as the
utility outfielder-coach read that certain letter in front of a
visitors' locker. He saw Umbric's eyes get misty although he
was smiling. He heard the player say aloud as he folded the
letter up and shoved it into his coat pocket, "The nervy little
cuss! He's a real tiger." And then Umbric suddenly swung
around when he heard Griff Holley's voice. "Griff, put me in
there tonight, will you? I could hit a Walter Johnson right
now."

"Sure, Nick. You take a goof ball?"

"No wonder they furnish oxygen here," Ray Scott, the
rookie infielder said. "I walked six blocks this afternoon and
it felt like I'd climbed Pike's Peak."

Jim raised his arms over his head and took a few deep
breaths. He felt a minimum of distress, and was sure he could

go tonight. The Colorado Elks were holding a convention here in Denver. There would be a big crowd, and a lot of them would be in high spirits before reaching the park. Tim Shea came over as he checked his spikes. "I know you're tough, Bruck, but Griff figures you need another day of rest. Lew's starting in left."

"The late papers said I'd play, Tim," Jim protested. They'll expect me to——"

"Your public, Jim? Well, they can ask for their money back."

While he watched the Hawkeyes work out, from the dugout, a few minutes later, the Denver Steers across the way were already sharpening their horns. "Come on out, Bruckner! Hey, Griff, trot the monster out."

Jim came out into full view, facetiously tipped his hat to the enemy, and brought a delightful, deafening response from nearly eleven thousand fans. He drew a forefinger across the front of his throat, and made a noise like a bawling calf. Hod Elmo, batting fungoes, swung his glance toward Jim. "Don't overdo it, Hamlet! Don't milk it." he shouted above the fans' racket.

At seven fifty-five, when the Steers took the field, the crowd was still griping over the absence of Jim Bruckner's name when the opposing lineups had been announced through the P. A. system. They got on Griff Holley. Was he saving Bruckner for the soft touches on the road? Jim sat on the bench between Hod Elmo and Ray Scott, a pleased smile playing at the corners of his mouth. Suddenly he shouted out at DeCorsia, on the mound for the Steers, "Hey, Vic, do you sweat gravy?"

DeCorsia looked his way and grinned.

"You're wasting your breath, Bruck," Hod said dryly. "That guy doesn't have rabbit ears."

Poke Hanna came away after looking at a third strike. Billy Koch swung at a two and two pitch and missed, and Jim leaned forward and watched Lew Paskert dig in against the

Steer's hottest hurler. "Hit it, kid. He's got nothing but a glove," he called out through cupped hands.

Five pitches later, the rookie threw his bat away, walked halfway to the dugout before going out to left, and yelled in at Jim, "You're right. I didn't even see the ball!"

Griff Holley growled, "He's going to be hard to take tonight."

The game developed into a pitching duel. In the fourth, Cal Kimbroch, after allowing a walk and the first hit for the Steers, left both runners stranded. The Hawkeyes did not break through on DeCorsia until the sixth, when Billy Koch slammed a single through the middle. After taking second on a fielder's choice, Koch died there. A fine running catch by Lew Paskert in the bottom of that inning saved Kimbroch from being scored on, and a smattering of Des Moines rooters in the stadium stood up when the Hawkeyes came in to begin the seventh.

DeCorsia got Lingersen to fly out to center, but Hal Rettig, after stubbornly working the string out, drove a fast ball just inside the left field foul line for a double. Griff Holley reached for strategy and sent Jim out to run for the catcher. He called Dutch Schaefer back and nodded to Nick Umbric. "Grab a bat."

Nick went out there and popped up to short on the first pitch. Coming back to the bench he grinned at Holley. "That wasn't Walter Johnson," he said ruefully.

Jim stood on second, taking the full treatment from the crowd and from the Steer infield. With two out, he took a big lead, shouting in at Faye Charlesworth to get hold of one. Faye obliged, hitting DeCorsia's third offering on a line to center. The Steer out there put his head down, charged the ball and fired it to the plate on the run. Thirty feet from home, Jim knew the play would be close. At the moment he hit the dirt he kept his eyes on the Steers' catcher's big mitt. He drove

123

his foot against it as the ball thudded into the pocket. The ball bounced out just as the umpire was about to give the "out" sign, and his momentum spilled the Denver catcher, Dakin, well in back of the plate.

Amid a cloudburst of boos and angry threats to his life that followed the "safe" sign, Jim got up and dusted himself off. He picked up Dakin's mask, held it out to the sputtering catcher, then dropped it as Dakin reached for it. Walking to the dugout he knew he had gone a little too far. Griff Holley's face was stony, his eyes looking past the man who had scored the only run of the game. The other Hawkeyes had been up and jumping when he'd slid across the plate. Now they were significantly silent. When Chet Kern made the third out, Umbric said, "That wasn't the least bit funny, Jim. It was insolence. Go look the word up."

"You got the run," Jim replied, his eyes smoldering. "Wasn't that why I was sent in?" He picked up a soiled towel and fired it out in front of the dugout, and suddenly felt an inner discomfort he could not blame on his bruised ribs. He set his teeth tight together, aware of a bitter taste in his mouth that did not come from his scrap tobacco. He felt like bawling.

He spoke to no one throughout the rest of the game, praying that the run would stand up. Cal Kimbroch, as if sensing his agony, turned back a threat in the last of the ninth and walked off the mound with a whitewash. Griff Holley was the first to sound off when the Hawkeyes reached the safety of their dressing room. "Don't bother reading the papers tomorrow, Bruckner. I'll give you the story now. 'Bruckner's taste as a comedian is below street level. He added insult to what could have conceivably been an injury to Dakin.' "

"Would any of you believe it if I told you I accidentally dropped that mask when I——"

"Would you expect us to?"

Jim slammed a spiked shoe down. "Yeah, I get a blast if I

124

do and I'm blasted if I don't." He picked up the shoe. "These spikes are sharp. Anybody want some of my blood?"

After he had showered and was getting ready for the street, he felt a slight nudge, and turned to see Cal Kimbroch's face close to his own. Kimbroch said, under his breath, "Thanks anyway, Jim," and moved away.

The pitcher's gesture put a warmth in him he sorely needed, and he was given an additional lift when the Des Moines writer, Harry Frankel, threw an angry shot at the Hawkeye players. "He's brought you guys alive whether you believe it or not. He finds ways to win ball games, and that's what they pay him for, not to establish palsy walsy public relations with opposing players."

Nick Umbric said when he left the dressing room with Jim, "Look out for Harry. He's quite a moocher. I'm holding a couple of his I.O.U.'s, if you get what I mean."

"Sure, I don't believe anybody, Nick."

Outside the gate, a group of fans, most of them teen-agers, appeared primed for trouble, and Hal Rettig, Charlesworth, and Poke Hanna quickly emerged with Umbric and Jim and ran the gauntlet of abuse to the waiting bus. A beverage can bounced off a policeman's shoulder, and a well-aimed apple spattered against the side of the vehicle, inches from Rettig's head. When the bus pulled away, Jose Acosta sighed deeply. "You know, I would be moch safer weeth Fidel Castro?" he exclaimed.

"This sure is like the old days," Griff Holley shouted from the front of the bus. "And you can have 'em!"

The Twi-Night double header started at six o'clock the next evening, Johnny Mundt taking the hill for Denver, to work the curtain raiser. The word that Jim Bruckner would be in left for the visitors brought an ear-ringing roar from the fans. With one out, Poke Hanna grounded out, Jim moved out to the on-deck station, and the thousands raised the roof once more. Mundt, before starting to work on Koch, threw him a curious glance, and Koch politely tipped his hard hat to the right hander.

Johnny Mundt had very prominent ears. Jim yelled out at him after Billy Koch let a low one go by. "How do you walk against the wind, Johnny?"

Mundt gave Jim an impersonal look, then got ready to pitch again. He pumped twice and threw a curve that Billy Koch nailed over short for a single. Number 7 for Des Moines received the greeting usually reserved for child-beaters when he stepped in to hit. Denver rooters begged Mundt to knock him down—to stick the ball in his ear—into his big mouth. Jim bit down hard on his cud and let Mundt's fast one buzz by. He fell away from a curve that broke in too close, then asked the umpire to examine the ball, and while this was being done, took a handkerchief from his back pocket and wiped the front of his shirt with it.

"Lay off, Bruckner!" the umpire warned.

"I don't know what you mean," Jim said innocently, and moved back in. He cut hard on a half-speed pitch and skied it to left, and as he made his way to left field, he got the full impact of the partisan crowd's hostile mood.

"How do you live with it?" Charlesworth asked before angling toward his position in center.

Wally Scherr lost no time in getting into a jam. The southpaw walked the first Steer he faced, then was gored for a double by the number two hitter in the Denver batting order. Hal Ginter, the Steers' shortstop, worked Scherr to a three and one count, then drove one high and deep to left. Jim turned and ran back, too far to his right. Reversing his field, he slipped, and the ball dropped in and rolled to the fence. Ginter was on third when he fired in to Poke Hanna, who had come

126

out from short to take the relay. Two runs went up on the board for Denver.

The razzing from the stands turned Jim's neck red: "Old Iron Glove!" "You couldn't catch a turtle with a butterfly net, Bruckner!" "I've got a kid in the Little League could have made that catch, you bum!"

Wally Scherr, after a long and hard look toward left, took a deep breath and went to work on the Steers' cleanup hitter. He struck him out, but the next batter drove deep enough to Billy Koch to allow Ginter to trot in from third. Dakin fouled out to Hal Rettig, and the Hawkeyes ran in, trailing, 3-0.

There was no change in the score until the fifth, when Lingersen poled one over the barrier in left after two were out. Jim, who had drawn a walk, scored ahead of him. The Hawkeyes trailed by the single run when they came to bat in the top of the seventh. "One out!" a stout-lunged fan behind the visitors' dugout hollered as Jim went up to lead off. The Steer bench got on him full force along with the crowd.

Jim let a slider go by, low and outside. He cut at Mundt's second pitch and fouled it high back of the plate. Dakin ripped off his mask and backtracked fast. As a brisk breeze carried the ball back to the screen, Jim suddenly got an idea. He dropped his bat and hurriedly retrieved Dakin's mask. Holding it tightly in both hands as if it had been a priceless Ming vase, he approached the Denver catcher. Dakin, his eyes both hot and wary, took the mask, then broke down and laughed.

Jim grinned as he picked up his bat. The crowd was laughing, too. He had made it plain that they could have erred in their judgment of him yesterday. "Bruckner," the Denver backstop said as he hunkered down, "you *are* a confidence man."

Mundt slipped a second strike by him, and he stepped out and gave the umpire that certain look. The man in blue said impersonally, "It got the inside corner. You check your eyesight lately, Bruckner?"

He got back in. The next offering was Mundt's half-speed curve and he hit it off the end of his bat and looped it into right for a hit. A few moments later, taking his lead off first, he simply could not understand why he had not rattled that pitch against the fence in right center. That ball had hung right in front of his eyes just begging to be slaughtered. He ducked back to the bag quickly when Mundt threw over. Well, a hit was a hit.

George Lingersen fouled a pitch out of the park, took a strike, then popped up to the Steers' third baseman. Hal Rettig, still swinging a red-hot bat, worked Mundt for nine pitches before he got hold of a fast ball and drove it out of sight. Running the bases ahead of Rettig, Jim wondered what had happened to his own extra base hits. Worry was plain on his face as he picked up a towel to wipe it of sweat.

The Hawkeyes continued to bombard the Steer southpaw. Dutch Schaefer singled, and Faye Charlesworth tripled down the alley between left and center. The Denver pilot came out to the mound and took the ball from Mundt. He brought a right-hander in.

The lights went on when the fireman was finished with his warmups. Chet Kern got the green light to hit at a three and nothing pitch, and he flied deep to right, scoring Charlesworth, and the Hawkeyes were out in front, 6-3. Jim did not see Wally Scherr take a third strike, His eyes were on Griff Holley, who was busy polishing his eyeglasses, and he felt a deeper irritation at the ceremony than he'd ever experienced before. Griff looked ten years older with the cheaters off.

Jim was the last Hawkeye out to the picket line, and a fan shouted, "Were you looking for a basket, Bruckner?"

Scherr, buoyed up by a three-run bulge, got the first two Steer hitters out on shots to the infield. When Jim made a

128

catch of a high and lazy fly ball, the fans accorded him a mocking ovation. On the way in he paused to doff his cap, a gesture that brought forth a ripple of laughter. He saw no evidence that his clowning had amused his teammates when he took his place on the bench. "I read your minds," he ground out. "You're right. When my old man got his first look at me he asked the doctor should he kiss it or kill it."

"It's plain to see he made the wrong decision," Hod Elmo quipped as Poke Hanna took his bat to the plate to start things off.

"One thing I hate about you, Hod," Jim said, forcing a grin. "I can't get mad at you."

The Hawkeyes rode herd on the Steer relief pitcher once more. Poke Hanna doubled, and Koch singled him home. Jim, up for his fourth official time at bat, smashed the ball straight at the Denver shortstop, who obligingly let it skip through his legs to ruin what seemed a certain double play. Koch held at second when the Steer right fielder lost no time charging the ball. Lingersen put the game beyond Denver's reach when he hit his second homer of the game, and twenty minutes later, the Hawkeyes, 10-4 winners, were under the showers.

Jim washed away his dirt and sweat but not his misgivings. He had pleased the crowd, perhaps, but certainly not himself. If Griff Holley was sending in reports on him to the Detroit front office he surely did not care to see them. Practically withdrawn from the jubilation that two straight wins over the Steers had injected into the other Hawkeye players, Jim combed his mind for the reason for his steadily dwindling batting average against minor league pitching, and his less than adequate defensive play.

He felt panic again. Even a patient man like Griff Holley would also want to know the reason if Des Moines slid into a losing streak. Roughhouse tactics and pantomime alone would not keep him from dropping into Class AA ball.

129

Tim Shea called him over to the rubbing table. "I want to take a look at your ribs, Jim."

He got up and slowly crossed the room, admitting to some misery in that part of him, too. Hod Elmo, looking on, chuckled. "If you could tear that patch off his ribs, Tim, and frame it, it would win first prize in an art show."

"I'd better let it alone," Shea decided. "It's healing fine."

Jim gave the coach-trainer a bland smile. "Look around, will you? See if you can find my batting eye."

Fifteen minutes before the night-cap was to start, Griff Holley emerged from his small office with a reshuffled line-up. Nick Umbric, the flexible veteran, would put on the catcher's gear, and Ray Scott would play at second in place of Dutch Schaefer. Jim, staring down at the floor, waited for the manager to name either Lew Paskert or Hod Elmo for left field. No further changes, however, were forthcoming, and he took a deep breath, got up and reached for a clean uniform shirt. An inner voice told him to be wary, for Griff could be giving him enough rope with which to hang himself.

His glance sought and found Lew Paskert, hoping to see a look of deep resentment in the bonus kid's eyes. But the kid was talking it up and laughing with a group of players in front of his locker. Yeah, Jim thought, all he has to do is wait a little longer. Those rookies were like vultures, waiting to pick an older man's bones.

12 ⊜

THE CROWD SEEMED BIGGER AND NOISIER WHEN JIM STEPPED
up to the plate in the top of the first inning of the night game.
Poke Hanna was on first by virtue of a walk; Billy Koch had
popped out to the catcher. The Steers pitcher, Cy Goomer, was
not too far from being seven feet tall. Jim, as he threw a loaded
bat away, threw the umpire a grin. "They should make that
guy pitch standing in a hole," he said.

Goomer's first ball hummed over the plate letter-high for a
called strike, and Dakin, the Denver backstop, held the ball
up in front of Jim's nose before throwing it back. In the wake
of a delighted roar from the stands, Dakin said, "Hope you
don't mind my gettin' into the act, Bruckner."

Jim spat into the dirt, dug a deeper hole for his left foot,
and waited. A pitch came in tight and tied him up, and he
was behind nothing and two. The crowd and the Steer bench
rode him unmercifully as he stepped out, seemingly baffled
by the big pitcher's wares. Set once more, he laid off a curve
that broke too far out, then a change-up that was too high.
The palms of his hands oozed sweat, and he reached for some
dirt. Standing in again, Goomer let him wait.

"Str-r-r-rike the bum out, Cy!"

The pitch smoked in, too close, and Jim ducked out of
the way, but the ball hit the meat end of his bat and arced out

into short right, out of the reach of the Steer fielders. Poke Hanna raced all the way to third, and Jim, holding at first, threw his protective helmet away and grinned into the storm of boos.

Lingersen's sacrifice fly to deep left center scored Poke, and Jim tagged up and tore for second. The Denver left fielder fired the ball in a line to second, and Jim, as he hit the dirt on his stomach, knew it had him beaten by two feet. Sliding in, he met the Steer baseman's hard tag with the left side of his jaw. The lights went out for a few seconds. Half-stunned, he lifted himself to his hands and knees and shook the haze out of his eyes. He looked up and saw Griff Holley and Tim Shea coming in on the run. A voice right behind him brought his head around. "It was an accident, Bruckner. Hey, you lost your chaw." The Steers' second baseman gave him a cold smile.

Jim got up, his fingers exploring for damage to his teeth. The left side of his face felt shot full of novocaine. He started to jog off when Griff caught him by the arm. "The ball bounced off your jaw, Jim. You were safe. You sure made it the hard way."

When Griff and Tim Shea trotted off the diamond, Jim whirled toward the Denver second baseman. A man in blue yelled "Knock it off! Start something, Bruckner, and I'll throw you out."

Jim laughed and moved back on the bag. "I just wanted to tell him his slip was showing."

Play resumed, Nick Umbric rocked Goomer with a double to right, and Jim scored the second Des Moines run, the Bronx cheers from the stands accompanying him to the dugout. Hod Elmo said, "You look naked without that cud of tobacco. That guy sure put the slug on you, Bruck."

"Yeah," Jim admitted. "How about a whiff of that oxygen, Tim?"

When Ray Scott struck out, Jim ran out to left field, getting

132

another withering blast from the Denver rooters. It brought a grin of satisfaction to the healthy side of his face. Thumbs down or thumbs up made no difference. They were aware that he was in the ball game. So far, he'd given them their money's worth.

The Steers, stung by two straight reverses, lost no time shelling Cliff Wrigley, Holley's pitcher. They eclipsed the drama of the first half of the inning with three singles, a walk, a double and a home run, good for six big runs. Tom Ellstrom took over for Wrigley, and Jose Acosta had to come in and relieve Ellstrom. Jose finally got the Steers corralled when it seemed Griff Holley would have to dig deeper into his bullpen.

The Hawkeyes were easy prey for Cy Goomer in the second. The Steers picked up another run, unearned, in their half. Jim came up for his second time at bat in the top of the third, and got more good-natured ribbing than abuse, and the fans, when he went down swinging for the third out, ignored him and applauded big Goomer as he strolled off the hill. Jim, after throwing his bat halfway up the first base line, made his way to the outfield.

Faye Charlesworth angled toward him, sensing his mood. "You're pressing, Jim. You're still trying to make a hit with the crowd instead of with your bat."

"Thanks a lot," Jim clipped. "Who asked you?"

Jose Acosta disposed of the first two Steer batters, then fed Dakin a pitch that the big catcher lifted into left center. Jim raced in along with Charlesworth, and heard the center fielder yell for him to keep away. His pride told him to keep going, but another big E for error flashed in his mind. He put on the brakes and let Faye have it. Reaching the dugout, he averted his eyes from Griff Holley, not caring or daring to attempt to read the man's thoughts behind those thick lenses he wore. For a reason he could not fathom, those eyeglasses had given him a feeling of depression for the past few days.

133

The Hawkeyes tried in vain to break through on Goomer, and when they moved in to hit in the eighth, they trailed, 11-2. Billy Koch led off and was thrown out, third to first. Jim, before he stepped up to the plate, swept his eyes over the stands, where hundreds of fans were moving toward the aisles. Those bent on remaining to the final out apparently had expended most of their lung power, for the reception they gave him amounted to little more than widely scattered boos. The Denver bench jockeys, however, could still be heard loud and clear. One tormentor with a booming bass voice yelled, "He isn't even a banjo hitter, Cy! He swings a ukulele."

Goomer lowered his head and looked in at him disdainfully, Jim thought, and he felt a surge of anger. He swung viciously at a slider and didn't get it, and a mocking barrage from the home dugout brought his rage up in his throat. The next pitch looked a little high and he laid off. The strike call spun him around and he shouted, "Are you nuts, Hibbard? Wait, I'll go get Holley's cheaters for you."

The arbiter whipped off his mask and immediately thumbed Jim out of the game, bringing the crowd fully alive again. The Hawkeye manager and George Lingersen, the on-deck hitter, finally had to pull Jim out of a possible fine or suspension. Escorting his player to the bench, Holley said in a calm but brittle voice, "It was a good call, Bruckner. Go cool off, but don't leave the dressing room, understand?"

"Sure, Griff, sure." The sweat on him suddenly became cold. Fear dogged him to the showers.

He was in his street clothes when the Hawkeyes came in from the field, stung by a 14-3 defeat. Griff Holley motioned him toward his office, and Jim gave Nick Umbric a dismal smile. "Ever ride the Paducah bus?" he asked.

The Des Moines manager said, "Sit down, Jim," when the ballplayer shut the door behind him. After a long uncomfortable moment he took off his glasses and tapped them against the arm of his chair. "I should nail everything down here and frisk you for a knife before I tell you this, Jim. A suggestion, rather. I've been watching you closely. There's nothing wrong with the way you stand at the plate or with your swing. Frankly, I think I've got the solution. You most likely need glasses."

Jim lifted himself out of the chair, his eyes widening, his mouth opened wide. A scornful laugh escaped him as he settled back again. "Griff, you have to be kidding."

"Far from it! Look, I didn't expect the Detroit club to send me a two-fifty-nine hitter, not one who plays the outfield like you do. And your shenanigans are beginning to weary the fans, believe it or not." Holley got to his feet and stabbed a finger at the outfielder. "I am not making a suggestion, Jim. I'm giving you an order. You'll have a complete eye examination when we get back from this trip unless you're hitting closer to two-seventy. That, or a ticket to a Class AA club."

Jim shook his head from side to side. He felt a terrible void where his stomach should have been. "Me, Griff? With cheaters?"

"You? Let me name you over a dozen players in the big leagues that wear them, Jim. Who do you think you are? What could possibly spoil the looks of your face when it's all pulled out of shape from chewing tobacco?"

"No sale, Griff. Watch me start hitting." He got to his feet. "That all?"

"For now."

Out in the dressing room he told a group of Hawkeyes what Holley had suggested he do, and then burst out laughing.

A week later, after going one for four in Topeka, there was no laughter in him. Des Moines had lost four out of the last six games and were bogged down in fourth place. The opposition was meeting his aggressiveness with aggressiveness, and the sports experts were bemoaning the fact that he was forcing young and clean-cut ballplayers to sink to his level. "Despite his limited talents, Bruckner continues to draw a certain element to the ball parks in large numbers," a Topeka writer wrote, "but we are certain that the average fan is no longer amused by his antics. Perhaps the Des Moines club could sign a sword-swallower or a fire-eater as an added attraction."

Jim, facing Topeka's southpaw, Jackman, in the first inning of the getaway game, was still nine points under a .270 batting average. The frustration of the past week had had its way with him; his temper was razor-edged, and his confidence badly shaken. The anvil chorus from the Chiefs' bench pounded in his brain as he fouled off the first pitch. Leading off second, Billy Koch, who had singled, yelled to be picked up.

He fell back from a brush-off pitch, then refused to bite at a low, fast ball. Jackman looked him over for fully ten seconds, then gave him a big motion and yanked the string on a curve ball. He cut far out in front of it for a second strike. He was certain the next one would be Jackman's hummer and he dug his spikes deeper into the dirt. It was another slow curve that cut the outside corner and he was waved out of there. He fired his bat away and nearly took the feet out from under Lingersen approaching the plate.

Griff Holley said angrily as Jim ducked in, "You watch that, you hear?"

The Chiefs picked up a run off Cal Kimbroch in the fourth to break a nothing-nothing deadlock, but Hal Rettig put the Hawkeyes out in front in the fifth with a blast over the right field wall after Lingersen had doubled. It was still 2-1 in Des Moines' favor in the top of the seventh when Poke Hanna opened up with a walk. Poke stole second just before Billy Koch popped up to the infield, and Jim was about to leave the on-deck station when Griff Holley called him back.

As he walked that awful "mile" to the dugout, it seemed that there was derision even in the announcer's voice. "Batt-

136

i-i-i-ing for-r-r-r   Br-r-r-ruckner, number-r-r-r   four-r-rteen,
Lew Paskert!"

The fans gave Jim no mercy. Many reminded him that he
was on the well-greased skids. A voice from behind the visitors' dugout, one that had rubbed his nerves raw all during
the humid night, jeered, "They'll like you in Split Lip, Idaho,
Bruckner!"

He lost control. He was about to climb into the stands when
Griff Holley and four other Hawkeye players moved out to
contain him. Hod Elmo, tugging at him, shouted, "You dish
it out, but you can't eat your own cooking."

A few minutes later he sat on a bench in front of his locker,
projecting his mind back twenty years. He was the bitterly
resentful kid back on Halstead once more, kicked off the street
because he tried to defend himself. He recalled all the old
grudges, all the painful lumps, and hugged them to him. Not
until he got under a shower-head did he wash most of the past
out of him. Nothing for three tonight with the bat. Tomorrow
afternoon the Hawkeyes would be home. Toweling off, he
laughed in disbelief. Griff must have been kidding. Jim Bruckner with glasses? It was King Kong in a pinafore.

The Hawkeyes were a happy bunch when they spilled into
the dressing room. Cal Kimbroch had scalped the Chiefs, 3-1.
Lew Paskert had driven in the insurance run in the top of the
ninth. Nick Umbric walked over to Jim. "You know, knucklehead, that Griff could be right. Something is wrong with you.
You're still too young to slip so fast without a reason."

Jim felt a stab of fear. "Y-you don't think, Nick, that I've got
what—you know—what Lou Gehrig——"

"Nuts. For Pete's sake, Jim, don't get a phobia."

"Me, wearing cheaters, Nick! I'd rather shoot myself."

"Two to one you'd miss," Nick said, and turned away.

The air-conditioned bus took the Hawkeyes out of Topeka,
the twin-engined plane having been taken over at Little Rock

137

by the owner and a group of his company executives. It was Thursday, an off day, and there would be no action until Friday night when Memphis came in to open a series. Looking out the bus window at the scenery slipping by, Jim dismally contemplated a seamier side of baseball with its tacky lodgings and unappetizing menus, buses without springs that could be mobile steam baths, and shower rooms where players had to queue up, Griff and Nick were out of their minds. He was just a ballplayer who had burned out long before his time.

In the back of the bus Chet Kern and three others were criminally assaulting a popular song, assisted by Jose Acosta with his guitar, and behind where Nick and Jim sat, Lingersen and Hod Elmo were discussing the recent All-Star game, Hod claiming the Nationals wouldn't have won if the Titan's Brossett had not been out with a bad knee. "And the big guy better mend, George. The Titans have dropped a game and a half of their lead."

It couldn't happen to a nicer bunch of guys, Jim told himself, and he hoped the proverbial jinx would land on the pinstripers with both feet. And then he was jolted in his seat—and not from a sudden application of the bus's brakes. The quartette back there was singing, "I'm Looking at the World Through Rose-colored Glasses."

Nick said, sensing his edginess, "A coincidence, Jim. It's not the needle."

The bus arrived in Des Moines at one o'clock in the afternoon, and before Griff Holley let the players pile out, he announced that there would be batting practice for one and all at two o'clock the next afternoon.

Three hours later, the phone's insistent ring shook Jim out of a nap. The voice on the other end of the line was Griff Holley's. "Jim, I've made an appointment for you with Doctor Charles Pendler at ten thirty next Monday morning. He's in the Drake Building. Better write that down."

138

"Yeah, Griff. How can I ever thank you?" He banged the phone back on its cradle, stared down at it for fully a minute as if it had bitten him. He crossed the room and looked out of the window, at a sign at least six blocks away that cautioned motorists to look out for school children. Hell's bells, he could read every word. He laughed jerkily. Perhaps all he needed was vitamins.

The Hawkeyes were at the ball park at one thirty the following afternoon. Jim was in his monkey suit and on his way out of the dressing room when Nick called him back. "They're playing a Little League regional championship game across the river at four," Umbric said. "The Moline Little Giants and the Des Moines Gems. My kid, Freddie, is pitching for the Gems. How about going over there with me after batting practice?"

"Why not, Nick? Maybe I could catch on with one of those ball clubs," Jim said.

Holley put his players through a workout in the batting cage that lasted until half past three, and when Jim and Nick reached the scene of the Little League classic, the top half of the first inning was over, and the Gems were at bat. The scoreboard had a big zero up for the Little Giants.

"Man, it's a sweet little playing field, Nick," Jim said, "How lucky can some kids get?"

"You ask Freddie after the game," Umbric replied, deadly serious.

Jim leaned forward and watched a little guy in a Gem uniform swing at a pitch and miss. The boy looked top-heavy in his head-guard, and his sneakers looked two sizes too large. Nick said, "That's Eddie Mosser, the catcher. He hits .328."

The boy ignored the next two pitches, then hit a two and one pitch through short, and scampered to first. The crowd gave him a big hand. The little shaver on the mound for Moline looked as cool as a cucumber. He reared back and struck out the next Gem hitter, and Jim had to admire his poise. The next two Little leaguers could not advance Eddie Mosser, and the Little Giants ran in for their cuts.

The Gems moved out to the field, their pitcher the last one to leave the bench. Jim rose half out of his seat, an incredulous expression widening his eyes. The pint-sized Gem hurler, on his way to the mound amid a great round of applause, wore braces on both legs. It was plain that he walked with some difficulty, but his shoulders were thrown back proudly and he wore a smile on his face. Nick Umbric turned his eyes toward Jim's and they were swimming with pride.

"Yeah, that's Freddie," he said.

Inning by inning, Jim's amazement grew. Little Freddie Umbric left the mound in the last of the fifth with a one-hitter, his team ahead by two runs. In the third he had run out a hit to deep short that had knocked in the Gems' first tally, and Jim knew he would never forget the way the boy had run that sixty feet. It had had to cause him some pain.

Eyes almost unbelieving, he watched Freddie Umbric retire the Little Giants in the top of the sixth. Two of the visiting kids had gone down via the strikeout route. He was still glued to the wooden seat when the victorious Gems were swallowed up by a delighted partisan crowd, doting dads and half-laughing and half-crying mothers. When he finally got up to leave, he discovered Nick had gone.

13 ⚾

JIM FINALLY FOUND THE UMBRICS WAITING OUTSIDE THE ball park. He put an arm around Freddie and said, "You're the greatest." A half hour later he was the center of a family circle, a new experience for him, and the cockles of his rugged heart warmed when Freddie asked for his autograph.

"They're wrong about you, Jim," the Little League player said. "You're not like they say you are."

After a light supper, Freddie asked to be excused. He had to rest and go through some necessary exercises, a therapy he had never neglected for a single day. Nick took Jim out in back of the small suburban home and gave him a complete profile of his son. "They told him when he contracted polio in his sixth year that he'd never walk again, and Freddie refused to believe them. Jim, you should have watched the fight that kid put up. It was all guts and determination. He fooled them all. He had those two strikes on him at the start and hardly a leg to stand on, but he hung in there and kept swinging. In five more years he'll have those braces off, believe me. He will be a big league pitcher."

"And if he doesn't?"

Umbric's eyes flared up. "Ask Freddie that. He'll take your autograph and shove it down your throat. You—how tough did you say you've had it? Nuts, Bruckner. Compared to my kid, you were born to the Astorbilts in a penthouse, with a silver bat sticking out each side of your mouth! At eleven, he's a bigger man than you are."

Jim felt a lot smaller in his clothes. "I asked for that, Nick," he said, staring down at the grass. A rueful smile flickered on his face when he remembered a saying he'd heard from somewhere. About a man feeling sorry for himself because he had no shoes, until he saw a man who had no feet. It occurred to him that Nick had prepared this object lesson in advance, and he had to admit it had put a dent in his defensive armor. By way of covering any outward sign of this he said blandly, "But I get the message, Nick. Tell Griff that."

"So that's the way you think it was," Umbric replied, a look of disgust on his weathered face. "A brainwash. What can you wash that isn't there?" He got out of his folding chair, kicked it over, and glanced at his watch. "We've got about twenty minutes to get to the ball park."

Before he left, Jim made sure to thank Nick's wife for her kindness toward him. Freddie made his way downstairs as fast as he could to wish both players lots of luck. "Hit a homer for me, Jim," he said, and Nick, on his way to the door, allowed a laugh to escape him.

"Yeah, you ought to get a jackknife with both blades missing for his autograph, Freddie," he threw back over his shoulder.

"Pa's always kidding, Jim," the boy said, chuckling.

The moment Nick made his appearance in the dressing room, the Hawkeye players swarmed around him, showering him with congratulations. Ray Scott and a few others said they had seen Freddie pitch the one-hitter on TV. "Watchin' him gettin' set, Nick," Hod Elmo said excitedly, "and stickin' his little jaw out before he blew the fast ones by 'em—well, I'll never forget it. I never saw more courage when I was on Pork Chop Hill in Korea."

142

Griff Holley, working himself in close, said, "The scouts will flock to Williamsport if he gets there with the Gems, Nick." He pumped the veteran's hand, then hurried over to where Tim Shea was examining a spike wound on Chet Kern's leg. Jim slowly pulled on his uniform, feeling a lot like an outsider who had sneaked into the dressing room. He talked to himself. He had to get that kid out of his mind. Maybe all the other little leaguers who had played against Freddie had involuntarily held back as far as all-out effort was concerned.

A painful sense of guilt began to nag him just as Harry Frankel and two other writers approached, and he lost no time taking his feelings out on them. "No, you vultures. I am not about to go blind. I don't intend to take up that feud with Gus Nethercott. There's your answers, so get lost."

Frankel's bushy eyebrows jumped. "Sure, Bruckner. I was at the Little League game this afternoon and spotted you. I was surprised you weren't on the other side of town umpiring a gang rumble."

"Some day, Frankel," Jim threatened, "I am going to choke you with a copy of your own rag!"

"Better not wait," the sports writer snapped, moving away, "you haven't much time left."

Only a fair-sized crowd turned out that night to welcome the Hawkeyes back home, and during the pre-game workouts it was glaringly evident to Jim that he was no longer the main attraction. Bruckner buffs seemed to have become a minority, and even the Memphis bench jockeys gave him the impression that he was not worthy of their full attention. They did not have to put their thoughts into words. He was a firecracker that had sputtered menacingly, and burned out. The fans' noisy response when the big guns, Lingersen, Rettig, and Charlesworth, hammered away in the batting cage was only too significant.

143

His critics opened up on him when he took his practice cuts. "No field, no hit!" a fan shouted from behind first, "Bruckner. You're stealing your salary!"

Simulated gasps of amazement came from the Grays' bench each time Jim connected with the ball, and the ex-Cougar's temper began to heat up. His swings used up, he got out of there and walked halfway to the Memphis dugout, where he turned loose an only too familiar gesture of contempt.

A Memphis player shouted, "Why, Bruckner, that was even beyond my expectorations."

The local fans' boos all but drowned out the laughter and shouts of approval from the less-cultured element, and when Jim reached the dugout, he learned that Griff Holley had made a change in the Des Moines batting order. Lew Paskert would be in left field. Trapping the manager near the water-cooler, Jim asked him in no uncertain terms how a man could add points to a batting average sitting on the bench.

"You won't lose any, either," Holley said quietly, and left the dugout for the conference at the plate.

Fifteen minutes later, Jim tried to show sympathy for the Hawkeye regulars when they came in from the field, already trailing by four runs. The Grays had shelled Pete Nicola, and only a twin killing with the bases full had kept Tom Ellstrom from an early shower.

Abendroth, the Grays' "stopper," got Poke Hanna to ground out, third to first, and he fanned Koch. Jim watched Paskert closely as he stepped in, only too aware of the ripple of applause for the rookie. Paskert jumped back from Abendroth's first pitch, a blazing fast ball, but it was a strike. He swung at a curve and fouled it off, then refused to go for a low slider. The Memphis ace fired the one and two pitch in, and Paskert stood there and took it, and was out of there.

"At least I didn't cost fifty grand," Jim commented, and gave Nick Umbric a tantalizing grin. "You're going to be

144

a lonesome man directing traffic out there tonight. "That Aben——"

Griff Holley cut him off. "You could root for the Grays better up in the stands, Bruckner!"

"Yeah, what did you cost Detroit?" Hod Elmo asked scornfully, "a pine-tar rag and a batboy?"

Regretting having let his wounded vanity show, Jim sat back and stared out at Tom Ellstrom, who was getting ready to pitch to Gus Nethercott, leading off the second inning for the Grays. The urge to ride Gus at this moment was not in him, and Hod Elmo quickly picked up the ball. "Hey, Gus, when are you fightin' Liston?"

Nethercott stepped out after fouling a pitch off and grinned at the Hawkeye bench. "What are you saving Bruckner for, Griff?" he shouted, "Cassius Clay?"

Laughter ran the length of the Des Moines bench, and Jim came off it as if it turned red hot. "You're yellow, you big bum!" He was on the lip of the dugout when Griff Holley caught him by the arm and yanked him back. The crowd was in an uproar, and a grin came to Jim's face when he settled down next to Nick. Now they knew he was still around.

Nethercott skied to Paskert, and Tom Ellstrom's "junk" retired the next two Grays. The game turned dull as far as the fans were concerned until the sixth inning, when Billy Koch got the first Hawkeye hit off Abendroth, after Poke Hanna fanned. Lew Paskert reached first on an error, and then the crowd came up screaming when George Lingersen tripled to right center. Lingersen was slow in getting up after sliding into third, and Tim Shea ran out, Griff Holley at his heels. It proved to be a mild ankle sprain, but the trainer took Lingersen out of the game.

"Go in there, Jim," Holley said when he reached the dugout, and when the fans saw Number Seven jog toward third to run for Lingersen they let him know he was no longer the white-haired boy. "He can't hit," a stout-lunged fan back of third yelled, "he can't field. Can he run, Griff?"

Abendroth held a conference with Nethercott before pitching to Rettig. With first base open, the Memphis manager signaled that he wanted the Hawkeye catcher put on to set up the possible double play. Griff Holley countered with a move of his own, calling Ray Scott back, and sending Dutch Schaefer to the plate.

Jim took his lead off third when Abendroth went into his motion. Schaefer checked his swing on a low, fast ball, then cut at a curve and missed. Keeping the ball down around the batter's knees, hoping to make him hit it on the ground, Abendroth finally ran the string out, three and two. Dutch hit the payoff pitch to not-too-deep left center, and when the Grays' picketman gloved it, Jim heard Nick yell, "Hold up!" but he raced at full speed for the plate after tagging up. Halfway, he put on the brakes, seeing he had no chance, and with the fans' rage pelting down upon him, he tore back to third. Nethercott, overanxious, fired the ball over his third baseman's head, and Jim whirled around and ran in to score, Rettig taking second.

The smug grin that Jim carried into the dugout was immediately wiped away by Holley. "That grandstand stunt will cost you just twenty-five dollars, Bruckner! Nick Umbric isn't out there just to get the air."

"You wanted the run, Griff, and you got it," Jim said angrily. "They never expected me to try it, and it shook them up. The fans don't seem to mind."

"Knock it off, Bruck," Hod Elmo said disgustedly, "You got away with murder and they know it."

"The only crime is when you get caught, Hod," Jim said defiantly.

When Charlesworth popped out to Nethercott back of the plate, Holley said, "Get the first baseman's mitt, Jim. Do the best you can."

Taking his position off first, he was a perfect target for the Gray bench. They told him ballplayers had to take turns driving the bus in the Saginaw League. And wasn't he afraid that Al Schacht, the Clown Prince of Baseball, would sue him for copying his stuff? Sure, he was a throwback, all the way to Class D. It was the boondocks for him. He tried to close his mind to the torment as he concentrated on the batter at the plate. After the Grays' shortstop, Cargill, sliced a foul just outside third, he caught Griff's sign to move back a few steps. Ellstrom, ahead of the left-handed hitter, threw one outside that was hit off the bat-handle, and the ball popped lazily toward first, where Jim caught it without moving a step. The fans and the Grays on the bench gave him a round of undeserved applause, and going along with the act, he tipped his cap.

There was no trace of levity in him now. More deeply than ever he resented the past and was fearful of the future, for it seemed certain that he'd lost all the skills he had possessed. The crowd was laughing at him now, not with him, and he felt sick. Baseball was all he had.

Ellstrom got the side out, and Jim threw some parting shots at the Memphis bench on his way in. The score was still 4-3, in the Grays' favor, when the Hawkeyes returned to the field a few minutes later; but in the top of the eighth, the Memphis pilot removed Abendroth for a pinch hitter, when Ellstrom walked two men after getting one out. When the hitter, Vince Gardella, came away from the bat rack, Jim ran to the pitcher's box. Hal Rettig joined him there, a question in his eyes. "I know that guy," Jim said. "Kansas City had him for a while when I was with Cleveland. Pitch him tight, and you'll get him, Tom."

"You'd better be right," the Hawkeye catcher said, and left the mound.

Gardella rocked back from Ellstrom's first pitch, and the

147

umpire called it against him. A chin-high, half-speed ball brushed him back, evening the count, and Ellstrom threw a piece of junk that broke in over the inside corner. Gardella hit it with the handle of his bat and looped it out to Poke Hanna at short.

Ellstrom looked over at Jim, nodded and grinned. He struck the next batter out.

Lew Paskert was first up in the last of the eighth for Des Moines. A chunky southpaw, Carl Zeh, had taken over the pitching chores for the visitors, and as he peered down the pike for Nethercott's first sign, the enemy bench jockeys worked Jim over as he knelt in the on-deck circle. "Cleanup man? Wow! At the dinner table or with a mop, Bruckner?"

Paskert swung at the first two pitches from Zeh and got only a piece of one of them. He guessed right on the next two deliveries, but flied out deep to right when Zeh threw him a low curve. The fans lustily booed Jim as he made his way to the plate. Fans near the Hawkeye bench railed at Griff Holley for not calling the hitter back.

"You call yourself a manager, Holley? That bum couldn't hit an elephant in the rear with a plank!"

"Two-o-o-o-o-o ou-u-u-t!"

"Your wife here, Griff? Send her up!"

Jim clamped his teeth down hard on his chewing tobacco, and sensed that Zeh would hum his first pitch right over the heart of the plate. The razzing from the spectators built a roaring fire in him, put a razor edge on his temper. At the moment he hated every man, woman and child who had bought an admission ticket to the park. Taking a full windup, Zeh threw his fast one, and Jim took a vicious cut and drove it just beyond and inside the third base bag. The Grays' fielder made a brilliant backhand stab, righted himself, and fired the ball across the diamond. The throw was a little low, but the

148

Memphis first baseman came up with it, taking a shower of dirt in his face as Jim slid hard into the bag. The "safe" call from the umpire brought the Grays' manager storming out of his dugout.

Jim got up, brushed himself off, and grinned at the first baseman digging dirt out of his eyes. He relished that hit more than if it had been a surprise legacy from a rich uncle. It quieted the Grays on the bench, and put a damper on the crowd's negative mood. When the Memphis manager was ordered back to his dugout, he took a long lead off first and began to harass the Grays' relief pitcher.

After Hal Rettig bluffed a bunt on the first pitch, the Memphis infield became wary. The first and third basemen inched in when Zeh threw his second pitch, a low slider that Nethercott had to block with his body. The ball rolled a few feet away from the plate, and Jim put his head down and raced for second. Nethercott's recovery and throw were both hurried, the Memphis keystone man having to go high before he could come down with the tag. Jim slid in safely, and the fans suddenly got with him. You can all drop dead, he said to himself as he cleaned himself off again.

A few seconds later, Rettig rifled a single into left, and Jim came around to score. On his way to the dugout he gave the fans in that vicinity a contemptuous smile. When Griff Holley said, "That was heads-up ball, Jim," he made out he had not heard.

The game went into the eleventh, all tied, 4-4, and Jose Acosta, now pitching for Des Moines, retired the Grays in order. Billy Koch grounded out to start the Hawkeyes' part of the frame, but Lew Paskert scratched a hit through the box. The fans came up off their hands when Jim stepped in to hit. Most of the crowd was imploring; there was only a sprinkling of boos. The batter's resentment stretched a little thin when he waggled his bat at Zeh. He looked up at Nick Umbric, the coach off third, making sure the bunt sign was on.

Zeh knew it. Most of the seven thousand fans looking on would have bet on it. Jim crowded the plate, knowing the southpaw would keep his stuff high. The first pitch came over, shoulder high, and the umpire yelled, "Strike!" Jim stepped out and gave the man in blue a shake of his head. When he got back in, Zeh threw over to first to keep Lew Paskert honest. The Grays' pitcher made two more attempts to pick Paskert off before lowering his head to study Nethercott's sign. Jim crouched over the plate, watched a half-speed pitch sail in, very tight. Although he knew it was not going to break, he was very slow moving back, and the ball grazed his left shoulder. The umpire waved him to first. Nethercott ripped off his mask and banged it to the ground, loudly claiming that the batter had deliberately tried to get hit by the pitch.

Zeh stormed off the mound, and the Memphis pilot rushed out of his dugout to back up his battery. Nethercott kicked dirt on the umpire's trousers and was immediately ejected. From first base, Jim taunted the Grays' bench, and the fans were ripping up the proverbial pea-patch.

The rhubarb finally over, Zeh, still steaming, got ready to work on Hall Rettig. His first pitch, wide of the plate, got by the second-string Memphis receiver, and the runners moved to second and third. The Grays' infield was moved in to cut off a run in the event of a ground ball, but Rettig tagged Zeh for a long drive that was caught close to the wall in left center, letting Paskert jog home with the winning run.

"You did everything but steal their watches, Bruck," Hod Elmo said to Jim when the Hawkeyes noisily filled the dressing room. "How did you do it without——"

"Hitting a ball out of the infield?" Jim interrupted, and gave Hod a sour smile. "My bat is only a prop." He angrily shouldered Elmo aside and fairly tore off his sodden uniform shirt.

150

"But you ask Griff. He's going to fix everything, Hod." Under the shower he thought of the two clean hits the rookie, Paskert, had made, and the two fine running catches the kid had made in left field, and he felt a few moments of panic. He felt ten years older than he was.

14 ☻

HARRY FRANKEL WAS A MAN WHO ALWAYS CLAIMED HE GAVE
the devil his due. He gave Jim Bruckner his share of the credit
for the Hawkeyes' extra-inning win against the league leaders.
"Bruckner's aggressiveness, if not a hot bat, led to two Des
Moines runs, and his 'accidentally' getting hit with a pitch in
the eleventh pushed the winning run into scoring position. Jim
got into the game when Lingersen turned an ankle in the sixth."

Reading Frankel's stint, Jim considered it little more than
a reprieve. He would take a .259 batting average into the game
that Saturday afternoon against the Grays, and more than likely
Griff would want to see more of Paskert and leave him on the
bench. If the kid kept hitting, he would be a cinch to play both
ends of the double-header against the Omaha Bees on Sunday.
He left the apartment and took a long walk, never having forgotten that old saying about a ballplayer's being no stronger
than his legs. They felt fine, so what ailed the rest of him?

Hours later, he sat on the bench and watched Lew Paskert
make a running catch that cut off two Memphis runs in the bottom of the second inning. "He can go get 'em," Hod Elmo said,
"but I don't think he'll ever hit good enough to make the
majors."

"You give me courage to go on," Jim said, a halfhearted
laugh escaping him.

It proved to be a bad night for Griff Holley's pitching. The Grays knocked Wally Scherr out in the fourth with four hits, two of them doubles. The game was put beyond the Hawkeyes' reach in the seventh when Nethercott hit Al McKim, the third Des Moines hurler, for a grand slam home run. A lot of the fans were on their way out when Lew Paskert came up to hit in the Des Moines half. The rookie worked the Gray's pitcher to a two and two count, then rattled a double off the right field wall for his second hit. Jim said wearily, "Maybe you're no judge of talent. You'll never be a scout, Hod."

"There was nobody on, Bruck. There was no pressure on him."

Paskert was left to die on second, and the Hawkeyes took the field again. Jim sat through the rest of the one-sided contest, his thoughts on Monday and what the day would bring. The scoreboard said, VISITORS, 12, HAWKEYES, 5, when Billy Koch made the third out in the last half of the ninth.

"Well, we'll get healthy again in tomorrow's double-header," Griff Holley said philosophically as he left the dugout with Nick Umbric. "We generally make honey against the Bees."

On Sunday afternoon, however, the Bees swarmed over Pete Nicola, the Hawkeyes' starter in the curtain-raiser, and stung him for three runs. By the end of the sixth frame, Omaha was out in front, 6-2, and Joe Acosta had replaced Nicols. The faithful stood up when Holley's players came in for their turns at bat in the seventh, and clamored for some base hits. "Put Bruckner in there, Griff," somebody behind the home dugout jeered. "At least he might get on."

Jim sat back on the bench, arms folded across his chest, a trace of a smile on his face. It was nice to hear the other Hawkeyes get sniped at once in a while. The fans began to come half alive when Poke Hanna wangled a walk out of the Omaha right-hander, Delaney, and they were up and clapping their hands and pounding their feet when the Bee shortstop bobbled

154

Koch's grounder. Lew Paskert, up for the third time without a hit, picked up the sign to bunt the runners along from Nick Umbric. He shortened up on Delaney's first pitch, waist-high, and popped it high into the air, the Bees' backstop taking it easily.

Lingersen, the big hitter, drew a round of applause as he dug in against Delaney. He had driven in the two Hawkeye runs. After taking a ball and a strike, he caught hold of a fast ball and rode it far out to right center, but the Bee center fielder flagged it down after a long run. The base runners moved up a notch, and were left stranded when Hal Rettig looked at a third strike. The Des Moines fans became even more dejected when the Bees scored two more runs in the top of the eighth, and applauded with a minimum of enthusiasm when Faye Charlesworth hit a solo home run in the bottom of the same frame.

The Hawkeyes retired to the dressing room beaten, 8-3, and Griff Holley lost no time shaking up the batting order. He moved Nick Charlesworth to the number three hitting spot, and dropped Ray Scott into the catcher's old slot. Chet Kern was given the Number Six position, and Jim soon found out that he would be playing the second game, hitting eighth in the order.

Tempers short, the players washed off and put on dry clothing next to their skin. Jim, after taking a swallow of Coke, called out to Cal Kimbroch, who was about to go out and start warming up. "We'll be a one-two punch, Cal. I'll get on. You belt a homer."

"I might just do that," the pitcher said. "I've had one during my seven years, and I'm due."

"Against Red Bennion, Cal?" Umbric fairly snorted. "He's rougher than Delaney."

The nightcap proved Nick guilty of a gross understatement. For four innings, the Hawkeyes got nothing that resembled a hit, and they trailed 2-0, when they resumed their swings

155

against the redheaded portsider in the last of the fifth. Dutch Schaefer, leading off, bent his head to the disgruntled fans' heckling, and proceeded to strike out for the second time. Jim moved out of the on-deck station, drawing an even worse reception. "You should've batted him tenth, Griff!" a rabid female fan hooted from behind the Des Moines dugout.

"Let it hit you in the head, Bruckner!"

The Bee infield anticipated the bunt, but Jim, after a ball and a strike had been called, laid down Bennion's third pitch. It was a lazy roller just inside the foul line, and the Omaha third baseman raced in to try for the bareheaded pickup. He missed, and the Hawkeyes had a man on. Here, Griff Holley faced a situation that never failed to turn a manager's hair gray. He needed a run, and he also needed Kimbroch's pitching. Finally, after the umpire's patience had run out, he called Kimbroch back, and nodded to Hod Elmo.

Holley's move brought a storm of boos from the fans, and it occurred to the manager that he had pulled a rock when Elmo slammed Bennion's second offering straight at the Omaha shortstop. Jim was forced at second, but he prevented the double play by bowling over the Bee second baseman. The man came up out of the dirt and lunged at him, both fists swinging, and Jim ducked low, got the Bee around the waist and wrestled him to the ground. Both dugouts were emptying when the second baseman gasped, "It's okay, Bruck, I lost my head."

Jim let the man up, and the crowd roared its appreciation when he slapped the fielder on the derriere and yanked his cap down over his eyes. A big round of applause broke out when he added his protest to those of the Omaha players when the second baseman was thumbed out of the game. "A great act, you phony," the Bees' manager shouted at Jim before he left the diamond.

Poke Hanna silenced the fans by popping out to the infield,

156

and there were very few bursts of sounds from the stands for the remainder of the game as Bennion refused to weaken. The Hawkeyes, whitewashed 5-0, were a dejected crew when they shuffled into the dressing room.

Griff Holley was in one of his infrequent bad moods, and he snapped at everybody within reach. He singled Jim out and said caustically, "That was a corny exhibition you put on."

"At that stage of the game I figured the fans should get something for their money!" Jim slammed a spiked shoe to the floor and stared Holley down.

Griff took his eyes away and heaved a deep sigh. "Forget it," he said, and sought the privacy of his office.

The writers arrived, Harry Frankel leading the way. Nick Umbric advised him to leave Griff alone. "What could he tell you anyway, Harry? We're not hitting. Our pitching is getting tired."

"I just have one question," Frankel said, and turned his attention to Jim. "What's this about some kind of examination tomorrow, Bruckner? Could it be for an acting part on television?"

"I'm gettin' tests for ragweed, Harry. And I think I'm allergic to you. You make one more smart crack and you will leave here with your teeth in your hand."

"Read me tomorrow, Bruckner!" Frankel said, his eyes snapping. He strode toward Holley's office.

Before they left the park, the Hawkeyes learned that Topeka had swept both ends of their twin bill with the Little Rock Travelers, which meant that they had dropped to fourth place once more. Further skidding, they knew, meant that changes would surely be made. They were also aware of the fact that the Detroit organization had issued the Des Moines front office an ultimatum at the beginning of the season. Unless a certain attendance figure was met, the working agreement between the two clubs would be terminated.

157

Jim accepted Nick's offer to drive him home, but he refused the veteran's invitation to share a steak with the Umbrics. "I'm going to be rotten company for myself tonight, Nick. What have you got against your wife?" He forced a laugh. "Imagine, an eye examination."

"Yeah," Nick said under his breath, "and I've heard a few people went through them before. Progress is remarkable, isn't it?"

The air conditioning in the offices of Dr. Charles Pendler, Ophthalmologist, Drake Building, was working perfectly at ten thirty the next morning, but the sweat flowed freely from Jim Bruckner. For a half hour he had been going through tests, peering at crazy-looking colored slides, all the while assuring the doctor that he needed glasses about as much as a snake needed shoes. Finally the professional man said, "I am sure I've diagnosed your trouble, Mr. Bruckner."

"How long have I got to live, Doc?"

Doctor Pendler grinned. "There's a long name to the disorder you wouldn't understand. It's simply a marked difference in the infraction of the two eyes. It is easily corrected by the right lenses."

Jim stiffened in his chair. "You mean glasses, Doc? Cheaters?"

"What is so terrible about eyeglasses, Mr. Bruckner? Thousands upon thousands of people wear them."

Jim felt sick. "I know, but—maybe I could get along without them."

"You're a baseball player," the doctor said. "You stand up at the plate with a ball coming at you very fast, right? If you don't get the full image of that ball when you swing your bat, you're not going to hit it solid. By the same premise, when a ball is dropping out of the air toward you——"

Jim nodded. He got out of the chair and asked, a lump in his throat, "When will they be ready for me, Doc?"

"I'll have them for you Wednesday, at three o'clock."

"Thanks." Jim moved toward the door, stopped and swung his head around. "You don't know it, Doc, but I'm already dead."

A few minutes later he called Griff Holley from a booth in a drugstore. "Look," he said, "It's all over. The doc said I have to wear glasses. Don't bet I won't pack up and leave town, Griff."

"Don't be a knucklehead, Jim. It could be insurance for you for the next five years or more."

"Let me warn you, Griff! If you or any of the others make any cracks or give out with a laugh when I show up wearing them for the first time, somebody will get belted."

"I'll spread the alarm," Holley said, and Jim heard the manager chuckle before he hung up. Leaving the store, he walked as if in a waking dream. Old Four-eyes Bruckner. Bottle bottoms in front of his eyes. He'd never felt more miserable since the day his father burned his fielder's glove.

On Tuesday night the Hawkeyes lost their fourth straight, losing to the last-place Little Rock Travelers, 5-4, and Griff Holley's thumb was close to the panic button. Jim took over left field from Lew Paskert in the sixth, and went nothing for two at the plate. In the ninth he misjudged a fly ball that led to a Little Rock score and he drew an unmerciful beating from the small crowd. Before he left the ball park, he told Griff, "I'll do anything now to get a couple of hits. They can even pull all my teeth out and cut out my tonsils."

"Yeah—we'll see, Jim," the manager said. "The axe isn't far from my neck."

At three o'clock the next afternoon, Jim sat at a small table while Doctor Pendler fitted on his eyeglasses. "I'll attach a flexible band on the arms that will go around your head while you're playing ball, Mr. Bruckner. You selected nice rims. Not at all conspicuous."

"Are you kidding, Doc? I'll stand out like a spotted dog on a red wagon." He swallowed hard. "Do I have to wear these all the time?"

"It's best that you do for the next six months at least. Now, take a look in that mirror, and I doubt if you'll fail to recognize yourself."

Jim looked. He shuddered, closed his eyes and looked again. "Who's the egghead, Doc?" he asked in a choking voice. "They're awful. I look like——"

"I'll tell you something, Bruckner, and since you're not paying the bill it can't be flattery. You look at least five years younger."

"Yeah?" Jim stared at his image for another half minute, and finally said, "I'll get used to 'em, I suppose, Doc. They say a guy can get used to hanging."

Dr. Pendler laughed. "I've watched you play more than once, Jim. Vanity doesn't become you. In a few days you will think you were born with those things on."

"You'd better fix me up a spare, Doc. Somebody's going to try and knock these off." He suddenly chuckled. "But it's illegal to hit a guy with glasses on, huh? I can sue."

He took the glasses off when he got outside the building, and did not remove them from their case until he was in the privacy of his own apartment. Here he kept putting them on and off, all the while talking to himself. He was no worse off than thousands of other people. Lots of ballplayers wore cheaters. But he was Jim Bruckner.

He could not remember an afternoon that had passed as quickly. Time fairly flew, and just before seven o'clock, having purposely reached the ball park late, he put on his glasses just outside the dressing room, and inhaled deeply. He walked in, slamming the door behind him, and all the noise suddenly stopped. As he stared defiantly at the weathered faces of his teammates, it quickly occurred to him that Griff had readied

160

them for the occasion. Shock, however, had its way with them. Hod Elmo and Hal Rettig suddenly bent their heads close to their knees, and their shoulders shook a little.

Nick Umbric broke the ice. "Jim, I wouldn't have believed it! On you they don't look bad at all!"

"It's you, Bruck," Hod Elmo said, bringing his head up, "Yet it isn't. You look—look like a scholar."

Jim was still unsure of the Hawkeyes' sincerity—the meaning behind their grins. Maybe he would still have to wade in on some of them.

"Yeah, a scholar," Poke Hanna agreed. "That means you got to become a gentleman too, Bruck. Those cheaters will look terrible with a chaw of tobacco."

"Yeah? Any more cracks? Get them off your chests now, you bushers!" He strode toward Lew Paskert and Ray Scott, and Lew said hurriedly, "I haven't said a word, Bruckner. What are you so touchy about?"

Griff Holley came out of his office, stopped and stared. "Well, Jim, they sure become you. I mean it. But I have to say one thing. They've kind of changed the Bruckner image, and let's hope, his batting average."

"I dunno," Hod said dolefully. "They're pitching Trotman tonight."

The Hawkeyes hurriedly finished getting into their uniforms, wasting only a few glances at Jim. As far as they were concerned, it seemed, he had been wearing glasses all his life. Well, one bridge was crossed, Jim mused, as he reached for his uniform. He still had to face the fans out there, and the enemy bench jockeys.

When he came into the dugout, Griff was sending Cal Kimbroch out to warm up. The manager said, "You can forget the pre-game workout, Jim."

He shook his head, and then a deep-throated voice came over from the batting cage where the Travelers were swinging away. "I don't believe it! I'm seeing things. Look, Joe, it's Bruckner wearing glasses!"

Jim came out of the dugout and strode halfway to the batting cage. He said to Benny Knauf, the Little Rock first baseman, "Yeah, you big ox! Want to try an' knock 'em off? Come on, any one of you frowsy-tailed last placers."

Travelers came out of the dugout. They stared incredulously and then began laughing and ribbing. Jim turned and stared up at the crowd, and was rewarded by a gale of laughter. Griff shouted, "They think it's a gag, Jim. The old act!"

The fans started buzzing when he ran out to the outfield to shag fungoes. The P. A. system announcer, blessed with a sense of humor, blared out, "Now, hear this! Jim Bruckner is wearing eyeglasses!" A deafening roar swept in and over Jim when he ran back toward the fence for a long drive off Nick's fungo bat.

The ball stayed very clear against the arc-lighted sky, and he stayed with it all the way, gloving it a foot from the barrier. Faye Charlesworth yelled at him, "You don't look a bit like Bruckner!"

Nuts, Jim thought. It only happened because the light towers are burning stronger tonight. Doc Pendler most likely splits fees with a head shrinker. Well, the cheaters gave the fans a kick, so maybe they were worth the dough they'd cost the club.

162

15 ⚾

"YOU LOOK LIKE AN OWL," BRONSKY, THE LITTLE ROCK
catcher, said when Jim dug in at the plate to start the bottom
of the second frame. "They for protection?"

He ignored the thrust, anxiously awaited Trotman's first
pitch. It swept wide for a ball. Bronsky said, "You're not
crowdin' the plate, Bruck. Let's get a shot at you."

Sid Trotman shaved him close with a high fast one, and
then got down to serious pitching. He threw his slider in, and
the nickel curve appeared in front of Jim's eyes as fat as a
corn-fed hog. He gave it a full cut and met it with the meat
end of the bat, and knew it was a long ball as he took off for
first. He saw the Little Rock center fielder turn and run for the
fence, and was halfway to second when the ball was caught for
a long out.

Griff Holley greeted him with a wide grin when he returned
to the dugout. "You got hold of that one, Jim. It's about the
longest one you've hit since you got here."

"They make that ball bigger since yesterday?" Jim asked,
and settled down next to Hod Elmo.

Schaefer, Kern, and Cal Kimbroch could do nothing with
Trotman, and the Hawkeyes returned to the defense.

Cal Kimbroch got touched for a single in the third, then
retired the next two hitters. Benny Knauf hung in at the plate

until he got his pitch, and he belted it high to left, close to the foul line. Jim raced over, anything but gracefully, the ball clear against the lights. He circled under it, ran back a few steps and made the catch. He'd had it all the way, but some clowning was expected of him. He laughed at the exaggerated round of applause as he jogged in with Charlesworth. "I was wrong." the center fielder said, "That was you out there."

"How quick do you think a leopard can change its spots, Nick?"

Both pitchers had full charge of the hitters until the last of the fourth. Lingersen, leading off, cracked a single through the middle; and three pitches later, Hal Rettig doubled to left and sent Lingersen to third. Action began in the visitors' bullpen when Jim, batting sixth in Holley's lineup, stepped up to hit. Heckling burst out of the Travelers' bench and from all parts of the stands.

"Take off the specks, grandpa; we know who you are!"

"You gettin' ready for the Four-Eye League, Bruckner?"

Trotman fired his fast ball over for a called strike, then failed to get a corner with a breaking pitch. Jim fouled a pitch off, then watched a change-up float toward the plate. He timed it right and drove it up the alley between left and center, scoring Lingersen and Rettig, and slid into third to beat the throw from the outfield by a hair. He got to his feet, took off his glasses and held them up to the light, breathed on the lenses, and then wiped them with a handkerchief. Nick Umbric, off third, shouted above the fans' delighted roar, "With a hit like that, you don't need the old act, Jim!"

Dutch Schaefer popped up for the first out, but Chet Kern drove the ball deep enough to the Little Rock right fielder to allow Jim to come in with the third run. Cal Kimbroch swung listlessly at three of Trotman's pitches, then tossed his bat away and strode to the hill.

Cal Kimbroch refused to let the Little Rock hitters break through on him. The Hawkeyes continued to hit. Trotman was driven out in the sixth when Jim ripped a single through the left side of the Traveler infield with the bases loaded, making the score 9-1 in favor of the home team. The throw from the outfield came into second base, and the Little Rock infielder's back was toward the plate as he took the ball on a fast hop. He whirled to his right and lunged at the base runner, but Jim was not there. He had put on the brakes a few feet from the bag, and before the infielder assembled his scattered wits, the Hawkeye base runner went in with a fall-away slide to his left and hooked a foot into the bag. Lingersen broke for home, and the Little Rock second baseman fired wild to Bronsky. Jim, the crowd in an uproar, raced to third.

On the bench, Griff Holley said, "I read about Ty Cobb pulling that play once," then grinned wide when the Little Rock manager hurried to the mound, and signaled for a fourth pitcher.

"Still the showboat, huh?" Umbric yelled to Jim from the third base coaching box, but he was smiling.

An hour later the Des Moines players were stripping off after the hitting spree that buried the visitors, 15-1. Jim sat in front of his locker still not quite sure that it had not been more than a beautiful dream. He had slammed out three hits and drawn a walk in five official trips—had driven in five runs.

The writers converged on him, and Harry Frankel, the most intellectual of the local press, asked him where he had found the spectacles of Dr. Cagliostro.

"I went to a guy named Pendler," Jim said, and the sports columnist laughed.

"Cagliostro was an old Italian alchemist and faker, Bruck," Frankel explained. "He was supposed to have manufactured a pair of glasses that gave him magic powers."

165

"Sure, Harry. That's what I've got. I gave Trotman and the other pitchers the evil eye," Jim retorted. "You couldn't believe, maybe, that I might be comin' out of a slump?"

"Give me a few more days, Jim, and I'll try."

"You'll see some pretty hot pitching the next few days against the Topeka Chiefs and Denver," another writer assured him. "DeCorsia, Mundt, Homier, and Ted Banta. You've had trouble with those guys."

"Yeah, Charlie. I'll bet you're a riot at a wake." Jim got up and turned his back on the press. A mirror hanging at the rear of the wooden locker caught his reflection, and suddenly he admitted to himself that he looked five years younger. Sure, and what was more, he felt as if as many years had been stripped away from him. Did a man's personality change along with his looks?

Nick Umbric's voice brought his head around. Nick held a baseball out to him. "The one you wanted to send to that eye doctor. All autographed."

Jim grinned. "I'm going to mail it to him, Nick. I'm going to address it to Doctor Cagliostro, Drake Building."

The Topeka Chiefs came to town, grimly bent on holding third place in the standing. They pitted their ace, Ted Banta, against Griff Holley's Pete Nicola. The southpaw struck out seven Hawkeyes in four innings, including Jim, and had not allowed a man to reach first base. Doubt beginning to nibble at him, Jim played a single into a triple in the top of the fifth and cost Nicola a run.

In the bottom of the same frame, George Lingersen reached first when the Chiefs' shortstop bobbled his slow grounder. Jim took over the on-deck station when Hal Rettig faced Banta. Rettig fouled out to the Topeka backstop, and when Jim strode to the batter's box, a fan shouted, "Put on two pair of cheaters, Bruckner!"

Banta laid his first one in, a sinker that was just above Jim's knees. Strictly a low ball pitcher, he seldom crossed a hitter up with a high one. Something told Jim that he was going to get such a pitch, and Banta came in with one across the letters that started to break when Jim swung from his heels. The fans came up with the rifle-crack of the bat and yelled themselves hoarse as they watched the ball clear the left field barrier. Jim, a wide smile on his face, ran the bases behind Lingersen. He ran from second to third backwards, paused at third to shake hands with Nick, then sprinted across the plate. Banta, shaken up by the gopher ball, walked Dutch Schaefer, and Griff called Chet Kern back and sent Ray Scott up to hit. Off third, Nick began to make the signs.

The rookie infielder dumped Banta's first pitch between third base and the mound and the southpaw raced over and picked it up, then dropped it. The Chiefs held a powwow on the mound, for Pete Nicola was a fair hitter for a pitcher. They elected to pitch to him.

Banta got two strikes over on Nicola in a hurry, then tried for the kill with his sinker. The pitcher swung and golfed it into short right for a Texas League single, and the bases were loaded. Poke Hanna, the greatest judge of a bad pitch in the circuit, worked Banta to a full count. He poked at the next three pitches and fouled them off. Jim cupped his mouth with his hand and yelled, "Keep pokin', Poke. Poke his eyes out!"

Banta fired a ball into the dirt that his catcher could not dig out, and Dutch Schaefer loped in for the third Des Moines run. The Chiefs' manager held up play and went to the mound. After the summit meeting, he elected to leave Banta in. No sooner had he assumed his pose in the dugout when Billy Koch ripped a single into right field, driving in Scott and Nicola. That was all for Banta.

The Topeka relief pitcher got Charlesworth to pop up, but Lingersen poled a triple to right center, scoring Hanna and

167

Koch, and the crowd was close to hysteria over the big inning. Hal Rettig ended the visitors' agony when he lined out to short.

Pete Nicola gave up two runs and three hits the rest of the way, and the Hawkeyes had scalped four Topeka pitchers for sixteen hits and ten runs. Jim visualized the next day's box score. In four official times at bat he had made two hits and had driven in two runs. He had scored three times.

Carefully, very carefully, he removed his glasses before he got under a shower-head, and placed them on the top shelf of his locker, far back. Lew Paskert brushed past him. "Look out I don't steal them," the rookie said.

"They wouldn't do you any good, kid," Jim called after him. "You don't know the magic words that goes with 'em."

Hod Elmo clogged up to him, "I don't believe a pair of cheaters can make so much difference this quick."

"I only know, Hod, that the ball would not be where I was sure it had to be when I swung, the past few weeks," Jim said, and went into the shower room.

Outside the gate a bunch of fans were waiting. A little man with a shabby sports shirt and slacks timidly approached Jim and held a baseball out to him. "It's the one you hit for the homer. I was at the gas station over there when———"

"Sure, how much?" Jim asked.

"What do you take me for, Jim? I just thought you'd want it. I'm not lookin' for any dough." His grin displayed gaps in his teeth. " 'Course if a Topeka player had hit it, it would have cost him."

"Sorry," Jim said, "and thanks." He took the ball and dropped it into his pocket, walked across a parking lot with Nick Umbric. "Imagine that, Nick? I never got anything for nothing. I had to fight even for what belonged to me."

"Yeah. You're seeing things different in a lot of ways. Jim."

When Nick dropped him off at his corner, he tossed the ball

to Nick. "For Freddie," he said, "I'll sign it for him the next time you invite me to dinner. Tell him he's lucky he got that trouble in his legs, and not in his head like I did."

"What was that eye doctor's name, Jim?" Nick asked laughingly as he started the car up. "Jekyll or Hyde?"

The Hawkeyes, on fire, went on to win six of their next seven games, and were only a game and a half behind the second place Denver Steers when they began a thirteen-game road trip. Jim had eight hits in his last twenty-one times at bat, including two home runs, for a .380 batting average since he had put on the glasses. Home attendance was breaking all records.

Following the Sunday afternoon double-header that completed the home stand, Jim went to Griff Holley's office. The Des Moines sparkplug was bewildered. "I tell you it's crazy, Griff. It's spooky," he said. "I'm not seeing that much better."

"I disagree, Jim. You were always a natural hitter and there had to be a physical defect somewhere. All right, doubt that optometrists have made great progress the last fifty years if you wish, but stay superstitious like all other ballplayers. Whatever you do, don't take those specks off. They've made you see more than a baseball clearer. You see the world differently, don't you?"

Jim grinned, and nodded his head. His glance swung to the group picture of the old Alley Gang still hanging on the wall. His eyes were narrowed a little when he turned them back to Holley. "If they were such fakers, Griff, why do you hang on to that thing?"

"Sentiment, Jim. Maybe ego. I like to be reminded I made the big leagues once."

Jim got up to go. "You're also a faker, Griff. It's a wonder it doesn't fall off the wall and hit you on the head."

169

The manager laughed. "I've been expecting it to, Jim. But I think you've found the last few days that you can please the crowd with a bat more than you can with a slice of ham."

"You're so right, Griff, but I hope there's a little of that old gang left in me."

Sitting next to Nick on the plane heading south the next day, Jim read Harry Frankel's latest column.

"Since Jim Bruckner got his sights lined up," the man wrote, "there has been no stopping the Hawkeye rush toward the top of the league. He is the bonfire under the other players, and if he continues at his present pace, the phones in the Des Moines Club front office will soon be ringing. The Cougars, bogged down in seventh place, are in dire need of a hot bat.

"The Titans are hurting. With only three wins out of their last six games, their lead over the Chicago Lakers has been cut to five and a half games. Perhaps a letdown was not entirely unexpected. The Titans may be giving too much time to off-diamond projects. They are susceptible to two occupational diseases, apathy, and the monotony that can result from too much success. And they could be depending too much on the legendary magic of their pin-stripes."

"Wishful thinking," Jim said under his breath, and tossed the newspaper into Nick's lap.

"Huh?" Nick queried, half asleep.

"The Titans," Jim said. "Even Frankel falls for that hooey. If their lead isn't big enough in about two weeks, they'll do what they always have, make a deal for a hot National League pitcher or hitter. Remember Mize, Sain, and Enos Slaughter?"

"I could care less," Nick mumbled, and dropped his head back against the seat pillow.

The drone of the Convair's power plants was an opiate Jim always fought against, for, strangely enough, his brief daytime reveries always carried him back to the old days. He left his seat and walked back to the tail of the plane for a cup of black

170

coffee, and found Harry Frankel there, joking with the stewardess. The writer turned toward him, all business. "Did Griff tell you Mort Goodwin was in the stands yesterday, Jim?"

"Mort G—? Oh, Sam Grayson's chief scout. The greatest judge of baseball flesh in the business, in his own mind. Why was he slumming?"

"Are you kidding, Jim? Goodwin gave me the snow job he was only passing through and had some time to kill."

"Look, Harry. You can quote me. If The Detroit club is thinking of bringing me back, Sam Grayson will have to see that niece of his to ask permission. And I would rather go right down to Class A than owe that dame anything. What's she got on the old man, Harry? Does she know where he buries his bodies?"

"Don't tempt me, Jim," Frankel said. "That would make juicy reading for my public. It would build up yours."

"I said it, Harry. Use it if you want. The Cougars aren't the only big league club in this country." He finished his coffee and crumpled the paper cup in a big fist. "If you do write it, make it clear that I have a lot of respect for Mike Strager, but do not like Bob Vick."

When Jim walked away, Harry Frankel said, "Whew-w-w-w-w!" and asked for more black coffee. "Get thee behind me, Satan."

That night, at eight o'clock, the Little Rock Stadium had its biggest crowd of the season. All that day the local sports pages had dwelt upon Jim Bruckner's new image, and the writers intimated that Travelers like Benny Knauf, Bronsky, and DeGrossa still had to be shown that Bruckner's cheaters weren't only a prop, that his batting splurge wouldn't end as quickly as it had begun. "He's a Cinderella man for the moment," one opined, "and by midnight tonight he'll take off his hitting clothes and turn into a ham again."

"It's box-office tripe," Griff Holley said, grinning at Jim,

"The Travelers' management has run out of TV sets and dishes. They're giving away pieces of your hide tonight."

"I'll try to stop them," Jim said, and reached for his package of scrap tobacco. Suddenly he changed his mind, and when he followed Nick and Hod Elmo out to the visitors' dugout, there was no swelling in his right cheek.

Lew Paskert stared at him. "You forget something, Bruck? You look naked."

He shook his head. "You got any gum, Lew?" he asked.

Griff Holley said dubiously, "I don't know, Jim. I remember how I felt when they really started streamlining automobiles. He stared out at Mike Halka, warming up for Little Rock. "The guy looks fast tonight."

When Jim went out to swing in the batting cage, the Travelers opened up on him with both barrels. "Hey, fellers," Benny Knauf shouted, "Mr. Cheaters hasn't got his chaw!"

A Little Rock quartette started singing, "Big Bad Bill is Sweet, Swe-e-e-t William, no-o-ow!"

Jim grinned ruefully as he rattled a pitch off the left field barrier. The chickens had come home to roost; he was getting back what he had given out to a little bespectacled kid many years ago.

"The baseballs you've been hittin' have had eyes, not you, Bruckner!" DeGrossa mocked.

The workouts over, the groundmen dragged the infield, and the crowd yelled for action. Five minutes later, Poke Hanna stepped to the plate, and Mike Halka disposed of the leadoff man with four pitches. Koch and Charlesworth grounded out. When Jim reached a well-worn spot in left field, the partisan fans lost no time reaching for their needlework. Jim, aware of the fact that this crowd had not come out in force just to see a tail-end club perform, doffed his cap and bowed to the boos and catcalls. With much of the derision laced through with laughter, he glanced over at Charlesworth in center, and returned the man's grin. Now Jim remembered what Mike Strager had said once. Or had it been Charlie Overman? Anyway it was something about clowning being O. K. as long as it was mixed with a fair amount of competence.

Cal Kimbroch stared out at him before throwing his first pitch to the Little Rock leadoff man. The Hawkeye "stopper" was also grinning.

16 ⊜

THERE WAS NO SCORE IN THE GAME WHEN JIM CAME UP IN the bottom of the second, with one out, and Lingersen, who had tagged Halka for a double, on second. "Hello teacher," Bronsky, the other people's catcher, said scornfully. "Look out Mike don't stick the old apple in your ear."

"Yeah?" the umpire said. "If he does, it'll cost him fifty dollars."

Jim laughed and looked out at Halka. The pitch came in, a waist-high ball that was not too much alive. Jim shifted his feet, swung, and lined it to the opposite field for a single, scoring Lingersen. Ray Scott, playing second for Holley, also singled, and Jim raced around to third when the Little Rock center fielder kicked the ball around before picking it up.

Chet Kern got a green light on a three and nothing pitch and rammed it past third, just inside the bag for a double, and Jim came in with the second Des Moines run. With one out, and first base open, Halka walked Cal Kimbroch to see if he could induce Poke Hanna to hit into the double play. He kept his pitches low, too low, and finally walked the third run in. Harv Kelsoe, the Little Rock manager, hurried to the mound.

A fireman came in, and Billy Koch managed to hit into the twin killing to end the Hawkeye attack. Kimbroch gave the Travelers the whitewash brush for the next four innings, and in the last of the sixth, the Hawkeyes broke loose again, scoring five runs, Jim's triple having driven in two of them. The fans, disgusted, sat back and turned most of their abuse against their own side. Many of them were already moving toward the aisles.

Jim suddenly said, "They ought to get something for their money," and Griff Holley's eyes quickly picked him up. Jim grinned at the manager. "I mean, Griff, they didn't even get a prize tonight." He felt the little devils inside him, prodding him.

In the eighth inning, with the Hawkeyes leading, 11-4, Jim came up for his fourth official time. With one out, he finally drew a base on balls, and then Griff Holley put on the run-and-hit. Jim went down on the relief hurler's second pitch to Ray Scott, who hit the ball straight at the Little Rock second baseman. DeGrossa jumped to the middle station to make the force, and Jim dumped him hard as he caught the ball. Untangling himself from DeGrossa, he swept a hand over his eyes. His glasses had been knocked off.

He was on his hands and knees, groping frantically around when one of DeGrossa's spiked shoes came down hard a few inches from his fingers. He found his glasses, half buried in the dust, when DeGrossa roared, "There they are, you bum!" He reached out for one of the shortstop's legs when the man made another attempt to grind the glasses underfoot, and spilled him hard.

DeGrossa flailed at him with his fists, and players of both sides swarmed over the infield. Jim, fighting back, planted a fist against DeGrossa's nose just as three pairs of hands began dragging him loose. Little Rock fans were in an uproar, screaming their approval of the violent break in the game's one-sided monotony.

The umpires and the police finally restored order, but when play was resumed, Jim, Griff Holley and DeGrossa were on

176

their way to early showers. A wide grin bisected the left fielder's face, as he examined his glasses for damage. "You see De-Grossa's nose, Griff? Like a ripe tomato hit it?"

Griff had to laugh. "You do it somehow, even if you don't try, Jim. Yeah, it was monotonous."

"Hear that crowd out there?" Jim said, beaming. "Still whooping it up. What's better for business than a satisfied customer?"

"Put the glasses back on, Jim. I can see too much of the old image."

The pennant race moved into August, and the Hawkeyes, after an eleven-game winning streak, rode over Denver and into second place, three games behind Memphis. Jim took a .357 batting average into Topeka the day after Harry Frankel wrote a column that shook certain Detroit baseball VIP's almost loose from their serene ivory towers. Jim got a phone call at the Sunflower Hotel two hours before he was to leave for the ball park. The voice of Bob Vick, general manager of the Cougars, came hot over the wire.

"You tell me, Bruckner! You authorized that story Frankel wrote? It's going over every news service wire!" Vick raged. "If not, we'll sue him and his newspaper for every——"

"Hah, it's only a continued story, Vick, from the one that Grayson and his niece never bothered to deny when they dumped me in Des Moines."

There was a long silence at the other end, and Jim thought he heard a sputtering sound like bacon cooking on a grill. Vick's strident voice blared in his ear again. "What's got into you, Bruckner? You know what this will do to your chances of coming back to D——"

"Who wants to come back, Vick? You don't really need me that bad? Tell the ladybug I do not chew tobacco any more, just bubble gum. And I hope you'll excuse me. I have to clean my specks."

177

"You'll regret this, Bruckner!" Vick roared cross-country. "I'll see that you don't play with any other big league club and——"

"Try it, Mr. Vick. Tell me on what grounds," Jim said, no longer laughing. "I'll be the one to sue, because you haven't a leg to stand on."

The phone in Detroit crashed down on its cradle. Jim was stretched out on his bed, wondering if he hadn't projected his new image just a little too far, when Nick Umbric came in. He sat up and gave the veteran the full details.

Nick grinned, and spread his arms wide. "You're in the driver's seat for the first time in your life, Jim. Who am I to say I wouldn't step on the gas if I was in your shoes? I wouldn't worry over any of Vick's threats, and Sam Grayson isn't considered the most beloved man in baseball." He sat down and studied his roomie for a moment. "But have you cut off your nose to spite your homely face, Jim?"

"I thought of that when I hung up, Nick. More than one baseball player has been tagged for the ashcan for daring to talk back to his master. My big mouth——"

"Keep hitting," Nick said. "Just keep hitting."

That night under the lights, Jim pounded out a double and two singles, batted in three runs and made a catch of a shallow fly ball that surprised even himself. The Hawkeyes won their twelfth straight, 7-4, and the next morning they boarded the bus for home to begin a fight for first place with the Memphis Grays.

An hour out of Topeka, Nick dropped a copy of the weekly *The National Sporting News* in Jim's lap. "Read what it says under Class AAA highlights, under the heading, 'Hawkeyes Riding High on Bruckner's Blazing Bat.'"

Jim read the brief paragraph. It said he had not lost his aggressiveness, but that it was no longer the bloodletting kind. Writers and fans had removed the "grandstander" label they had affixed to him earlier in the season. He was Griff Holley's take-charge guy, a cinch to return to the majors.

Frankel came by when he tossed the paper back to Nick. "It just came over Chet Kern's transistor, "the writer said, "That Detroit tried to swing a deal with the Chicago Bruins but it fell through. Vick offered a first-line pitcher and Zach Jones for the Bruins' Joe Walzec."

"They must be hurting," Nick said. "I'm sure Joe is thirty-seven if he's a day."

"Seems they're not looking your way," Frankel said to Jim. "Well, you almost begged me to write that story."

"Who's crying, Harry?" Jim asked, forcing a smile. A few miles farther on he sought Tim Shea out and asked the trainer if he had anything in his bag that could quiet a fluttery stomach.

The Des Moines ball park was filled to more than capacity the following night when the leadoff man for Memphis moved in to hit against Pete Nicola. Pennant-hungry fans gave Jim a great ovation as he took his place in left field. They cheered every pitch Nicola made as he retired the visitors in order, and clamored for the Memphis pitcher's, Billy Abendroth's, blood when the Hawkeyes trotted in to take their cuts.

Abendroth put a silencer on the noisy crowd by striking out both Poke Hanna and Billy Koch. Faye Charlesworth flied out to left, and then the game evolved into a nerve-wracking pitcher's duel that found the scoreboard all goose eggs up to the last of the seventh. Lingersen, overdue, finally smashed a single into right, and the crowd rose up, screaming for Hal Rettig to keep it going.

The Hawkeye catcher, after swinging from his heels on the first pitch, shortened up and dumped Abendroth's second offering to the box. Abendroth whirled and forced Lingersen at second, but Rettig, fast for a catcher, beat the throw to first. Jim walked to the plate, the fans letting him hear what they expected of him loud and clear. Twice he had lined out deep to the outfield.

Gus Nethercott, back of the plate, tried to put a match to the old feud. "There's a fly on your specks, egghead. That's all you'll hit."

"Yeah? Your old man's mustache, Gus!" Jim clamped his hard hat down more firmly on his head and dug himself a foothold in the batter's box. Abendroth jammed him a little too close with a fast ball, and after checking Rettig, hovering off first, the Grays' ace southpaw turned loose a slider. Jim watched it like a hawk as it came in, took his full cut and drove it on a line down the alley between center and right. Rettig raced all the way home, and Jim pulled up at third with a triple. Bedlam broke loose in the stands.

Dutch Schaefer, back in the lineup, worked Abendroth to a full count and set the crowd wild once more with a high fly to deep left that allowed Jim to romp in with the Hawkeyes' second run. Chet Kern grounded out to end the inning.

The Grays fought back in the top of the ninth, and tied the score with a walk and three singles, and the fans, somewhat apprehensive and lung-weary, implored the Hawkeyes to manufacture a run when they trotted in to the dugout.

Charlesworth, leading off, lined straight into the Memphis shortstop's glove, but three pitches later, Lingersen blooped one to right that fell just inside the foul line for a single. While the fans applauded Jim to the plate, Gus Nethercott went out to the mound for a conference with Abendroth. A fan near the home bench shouted, "They'll walk him, the bums!"

"I don't think so," Griff Holley said to Tim Shea in the dugout. "It'll push the lead run to second and Dutch has always hit Billy pretty good."

Abendroth did pitch to the Hawkeye left fielder. He blew a knee-high strike past Jim, then elected to repeat the pitch. Jim swung and met it on the fat end of his bat, and the ball sailed out to left center, hit the scoreboard and bounced off. Hal Rettig, running as if chased by a hungry pack of wolves, was waved around third by Nick Umbric. The relay was wide of the plate and Rettig slid across before a tag could be made. Throwing away all restraint, the fans spilled out of the stands and onto the playing field. Jim had to literally fight them off as he tore for the dressing room.

He was the last one in. The left sleeve of his uniform shirt had been nearly torn from his shoulder, and there was a smear of lipstick on his sweaty face. Pete Nicola hooked an arm around his neck and shouted, "You old crowd-pleaser!" The other players milled around him and he waved them off.

There was an insistent pounding on the door, and Griff Holley opened it a crack and peered out. "Let them wash up and get a breath, you buzzards!" he yelled at the writers. "Give them ten minutes!"

Harry Frankel had news for Jim. Bob Vick had made a statement to the Transcontinental Press. "He said your old grudge against the Cougars is unwarranted and ridiculous, that you're still playing to the public. He also said you still fitted into the Detroit club's plans."

"Hooray for him," Jim snorted. "Has anybody ever talked to Mike Strager?"

Frankel nodded. "There was an observation by Mike tacked on to the same story! 'I'd rather have a contented two-sixty hitter than a dissatisfied three hundred and sixty hitter.' "

"Good old honest Mike," Jim said, and shook his head. "Well, Des Moines isn't such a bad little town. I might build a home here."

The bolt came out of the blue the next afternoon. Jim had no sooner turned on the radio to get a few innings of the Detroit-Chicago day game when the announcer said, ". . . Mike Strager's contract has another year to run, and no doubt he will collect his salary in full. Bob Vick intimated that

181

further changes will be made in the Cougars, now bogged down in seventh place. Until a new manager is selected, Coach Josh Dillon will run the club. Mike Strager came to Detroit from . . ."

Jim silenced the set with a vicious twist of the dial, suddenly aware of the transitory existence of the pro ballplayer, his susceptibility to the politics and whims of a front office. They can easily mark a man as dead while he's fully alive. He looked into the mirror and told himself he was just looking at a minor league ballplayer who had been hitting minor league pitchers, and he felt scared, even with his glasses on.

Jim was lacing up a spiked shoe that night when Tim Shea handed him a telegram. "Just got here, Jim," the trainer said.

It was from Mike Strager. It said: SIT TIGHT AND KEEP YOUR MOUTH SHUT STOP I KNOW WHAT I KNOW. MIKE.

Two hours later, Jim's third single in the eighth inning put the Hawkeyes two runs ahead of the Grays, 6-4, and Wally Scherr made the lead stand up the rest of the way. Griff Holley caught Jim by the arm when his red-hot players reached the dressing room. "I thought that news about Mike would have you down tonight, Jim. You acted just the opposite."

Jim threw a sodden sweat shirt into a hamper. He gave Holley his biggest grin. "Just say I know what I know, Griff, and the truth is I don't know a thing. After all, I am way out in left field."

"Thank heavens," the manager said as he walked off, "there is some screwball left in you."

17 ⚾

THE CENTRAL LEAGUE PENNANT RACE RUSHED CLOSE TO
September. The Hawkeyes, paced by Jim Bruckner's .351
batting average, rode in and over Memphis by three and a
half games by the time Griff Holley's players were to board
the big bus for a short road trip, their last one.

In the Majors, the Cleveland Braves were making their
bid, and were only five games behind the worried Titans. The
Detroit club had called up a pitcher and a .301 hitter from
their farm system, and when the news had reached Jim, he'd
asked Nick, "How about it? Can I yell, 'Sell me or bring me
up' ?"

Under the arc lights in Topeka, his resentment against the
Cougars steadily built up. Gibes from the enemy bench began
to get under his skin for the first time in weeks. "You're an
unwanted child, Bruck! You'll never get out of Siberia!" one
shouted at him when he came up to hit in the bottom of the
second inning. He lashed out at a three and one pitch and
smashed it through the middle, nearly taking the Chief pitcher's legs out from under him. With Dutch Schaefer up, he
stole second, hitting the dirt with his spikes high, and bringing
a howl of anger and pain from the Topeka second baseman.
Time was called when the home club's trainer came out.

Jim turned a deaf ear to enemy threats as he cleaned himself of dirt. At the moment he was his old self, grateful for his improved eyesight only because it gave him a clearer shot at the world. He grinned at the booing crowd.

Schaefer grounded out to the right side, and Jim ran to third, to score a few moments later when Chet Kern skied out deep to right center. Griff Holley said when Jim reached the bench, "You're going blind again."

"Everything is very plain to me, Griff," Jim groused. "Even baseball has a leper colony." He snatched up his glove from the steps of the dugout when Cal Kimbroch struck out.

Up in the press box at the end of the sixth inning, Harry Frankel typed out copy for the next day's editions. "Bruckner's second hit of the game, a double to the right field wall, drove in Koch and Rettig to give the Hawkeyes a 7-2 lead. This gives the bespectacled slugger a total of 67 runs batted in since joining the club. He's still the hungry ballplayer; a lot of the old breed is still in his blood. He'll beat the opposition in a dozen ways. . . ."

In the hotel room that night, Jim asked Umbric, "How does my satisfied face look without a nose, Nick?"

"You won't get it through your thick skull, will you, Jim? Des Moines is close to its first pennant in seven years, and do you think Detroit will yank you out of the lineup now? They aren't going anywhere. I'll bet my house and lot you'll be at Mesa with the Cougars come spring."

"I never bet, Nick. I've been a loser too many times."

"Sure. Because you wanted to be," Nick replied with an impatient flip of a hand. "Knock it off. I want some sleep."

After breakfast the next morning, Jim read a piece of baseball news that both disturbed and excited him. During yesterday afternoon's Cougar-Titan game in Detroit, Jeremiah Jones had fallen making a diving catch and had broken his collarbone. The colored outfielder would be out for the rest of the season. Jim sat down in an isolated corner of the lobby, and

184

considered. Detroit had to have outfield help. Lorber, the bonus kid, who had been alternating between first base and left field, had a batting average of .219. It was in Jim's mind that the fans in Detroit must have been putting some pressure on Bob Vick. Even in Class AAA, .360 hitters were few and far between.

Wally Scherr, with help from Tom Ellstrom and Jose Acosta, managed to pull a 7-6 squeaker out of the fire that night, Jim chipping in with two hits. They boarded the bus the next morning, bound for Omaha for a weekend stand of three games.

They arrived in the packing city in time for lunch, and Hod Elmo, sitting at a table in the hotel dining room with Jim, Faye Charlesworth and Nick Umbric, read a squib of news aloud from the *Omaha Times-Trib*. "The Cougars brought up Jimmy Robertson, a twenty-year-old outfielder, who hit .334 in the Prairie League."

Jim's appetite suddenly left him. He wished he had never heard of a chew of tobacco, and rued the fact that his tongue had always been faster than his brain. "You think they've got wheelchairs handy?" he asked Hod. "I doubt if I can make it to the elevator. Maybe Tim Shea carries Geritol."

"Well, it always was a kid's game," Hod said philosophically, and Jim got up and left.

The racket of a big Saturday night crowd shouldered along the sides of the dressing room when the Hawkeyes began suiting up. Bitter and on edge, Jim tested the sharpness of his spikes, determined to show the buffs out there more than a trace of his old image. Tim Shea approached him. "Jim, Griff wants you in his office."

He took his time. When he shut the door of the little cubicle behind him, the manager said without preliminaries, "Jim, you're leaving us. You'll be taking off at noon tomorrow."

Jim needed a full minute to recover from the shock of

Holley's announcement. A smile spreading slowly over his face, he said, "Well, I'll be willing to meet Vick halfway, let bygones be——"

Griff shook his head. "You're not reporting to the Cougars. You're going to the Titans. Detroit traded you and pitcher Ed Stangaard to New York for Joe Lubec and a player from the Titan farm system to be named later."

Jim's eyes seemed about to pop through his eyeglasses, and his heart skipped a couple of beats. An exclamation of surprise stuck in his throat, and he was certain he had heard wrong. Such a thing was not possible. Holley went on, his voice sounding far away, "The deal's been stewing for quite some time. Congratulations, Jim."

He reacted like a mechanical man when Holley extended a hand. "Let me sit down, Griff," he finally managed to say, and dropped slowly into a chair. He was a New York Titan, a pin-striper! He was with a first place club rated better than eight to five to get into the World Series. He would play with stars like Brossett, Sam Ricci, Ridel and Parisi. He was on baseball's Everest. A guy could go no higher.

"Jim, you've been trying to lick that bright pin-stripe world instead of joining it," Griff Holley said. "You never really hated most of the opposition. You envied it." He laughed. "Now you have the competence, remember this. In New York they like a little ham on rye. Phipps wants you there by noon on Monday."

All during that night game the fans applauded every move he made, in the field and at the plate. At bat in the seventh, with Rettig waiting to be picked up at second, the last twenty years of his life came into focus. Why, he'd never really been alone. He'd been too blind to see that. . . . He let an outside pitch go by. . . . Doc Pendler was not the only one who had helped him see things straight. There had been Mike Strager, Jeremiah Jones and Charlie Overman. . . . He

186

swung at a half-speed curve and fouled it into the stands.

. . . There was Nick Umbric and his amazing little guy, Freddie . . . and Griff. . . . He got the pitch he liked and rode it into right field, driving Rettig in with the Hawkeyes' sixth run. Taking a wide turn around first, he had no misgivings at all about staying with the Titans.

Leading off the bag, he knew what he was going to do after the fall classic. He'd write Charlie Overman and ask him if he could use a pin-striper to help with those kids at the baseball camp. Some of them might be mixed up in their thinking, and one or two might need eyeglasses. Yes, man, that was exactly what he was going to do, he told himself, just as Dutch Schaefer rifled a long ball to deep right center beyond the reach of the Bee pickets.

A big smile on his face, fully reflecting his new image, Jim tore around second. First, though, he'd go back to a certain section of Chicago and pick out a pair of promising-looking kids. It shouldn't cost too much at Vogel's baseball clinic. Anyhow, did the pin-stripers worry about money?

"You've got the green light, Jim!" Nick Umbric shouted as he rounded third.

"I know where I'm going, Nick!" he yelled back at the coach, and headed for home.

ABOUT THE AUTHOR

JOE ARCHIBALD began his writing career at the age of fifteen with a prize-winning contribution to the *Boston Post*. At twelve, he had submitted and sold his first cartoon to the original *Judge* magazine. He is a graduate of the Chicago Academy of Fine Arts.

During World War I, he served on a U.S. Navy sub-chaser and was staff cartoonist for a service publication. After the armistice he was a police and sports reporter for Boston newspapers, and then became a sports and panel cartoonist for the McClure Newspaper Syndicate in New York. Free-lancing since 1929, he has written countless stories and articles for boys on sports, aviation and adventure. With the outbreak of World War II, Joe Archibald became a cartoonist for the American Theatre Wing, and went overseas as a field director for the Red Cross.

His first book, published in 1947, won for him an enthusiastic following of young readers throughout the country, and the books he has written since then have proved his popularity with sports-minded boys.

He is a member of the National Cartoonist Society, has exhibited water colors, and is a director of amateur musical shows. He lives in Port Chester, New York, and is very active in community affairs.